Pussy Willow

TATIANA STRAUSS

Other Books By The Author

D o g R o s e

B l u e S p e e d w e l l

Copyright © Tatiana Strauss 2021
Tatiana Strauss has asserted her right to be identified as the author
of this work under the Copyright, Design and Patents Act 1988
This book is sold subject to the condition that it shall not,
by way of trade or otherwise, be lent, resold, hired out, or otherwise
circulated without the publisher's prior consent in any
form of binding or cover other than that in which
it is published and without a similar condition,
including this condition, being imposed
on the subsequent purchaser

This book is a work of fiction. Any resemblance to persons, living or dead,
events or locales is entirely coincidental

All rights reserved. No part of this publication may be reproduced,
distributed, or transmitted in any form or by any means, including
photocopying, recording, or other electronic or mechanical methods, or
by any information storage and retrieval system without the prior written
permission of the publisher, except in the case of very brief quotations
embodied in critical reviews and certain other non-commercial uses
permitted by copyright law. Any person who does any unauthorised
act in relation to the publication may be liable to criminal
prosecution and civil claims for damages

Cover photograph by Maria Matheou

Visit www.tatianastrauss.com to find out more about the
author. You will also find news of any author
events and you can sign up for e-newsletters so that
you are always first to hear about new releases

Follow Tatiana on Instagram: tatiana_strauss_author

Acknowledgments

My loving appreciation and thanks to Sarah for your eternal friendship, play, belief in my human expression and your limitless love. So many thank yous, Maria, for your love, your contributions, for your constancy, fun and so much more. To Mandi, to GlenRay, to Amelia, thank you for being all that you are in my life. To Katharine, and Nicci too, you who came along later to walk the walk with me. To every friend who cheered and supported me and read me along the way, my heartfelt thank you. Thank you dearly to Barry, who saluted me in everything I am, who was here from the beginning of my path as a writer—and so many more beginnings—you mysteriously took off—god, that hurt—and god, I've grown—but you're always here and your mark is forever in my life and in my work. Thank you to my mama, who was the maker of my own human beginning. To my papa. And my siblings—to Vanessa in particular, for you know why. My thanks to Jean McNeal and Giles Foden for encouraging me in the early days of the novel which was to become this series. To UEA. To John Boyne and Henry Sutton. To Ivan Mulcahy. To Broo Doherty. Thank you to Kosta Ouzas, Tamsyn Bester, Alex and the team at SPH. Thanks to Henry Glover. To Grace Mattingly.

To Dani Zargel. A huge thank you for the teachings and inspirations of the Buddha and the many teachers thereof; to Abraham Hicks for inspiring me via your extensive YouTube presence and teachings, also for your book, *Ask and it is Given*; to Eckhart Tolle for *The Power of Now*; to Anita Moorjani for sharing your NDE in interviews about your book, *Dying to be Me*. Thank you to Aaron Abke for your extraordinary gift of articulating a myriad spiritual teachings, and for resonating into my life in the last moments of my final edit of this book. Thank you to all and everyone who inspired me—on purpose or otherwise—who supported me; who led me to grow by shadow or by light; to all those I have loved, still love, and those who loved me or love me still…appreciation lives in me for you all.

PussyWillow

A Skinny Long-Stemmed Dandelion

His arms were wrapped around me in a slack kind of a hug, me lying all half over him, but when the big noise of the bug zoned in on us, he grew taut-as, gripped me too tight. The wind went insane, I could hear the water churning as a whole lot of force came swelling up from the lake. The little rowing boat got to feel like it was about to take off, all like Dorothy's house in The Wizard of Oz. I pictured us whizzing across the brightest-blue sky, the waves smacking ever harder against the boat's flimsy sides, cold splashes coming sharp as needles into my face. My whole instinct was urging me to check it out, but I knew I had to wait, went on feigning sleep, the squall pressing in on us like some kind of lead was in it. He muttered something, all drowned out by the drum of the whirring blades, the machine right above us now, so I felt I was being pancaked into him. I could hardly breathe from the pressure. A crazy thrill came sprinting into my chest.

I got to realise I was never going to hear anything, so I waited a few more seconds—then went for it, opened my eyes—and straight away it seemed like my eyeballs might just dry up. Or even get sucked right out of their sockets. But I kept going, pushed myself up with the flat of my hand against his chest—forced him to release me, as he went right on being asleep. The helicopter lowered some, like maybe it was going to land on us, and the wooden dinghy started swivelling, at the same time pitching all over the place. I saw how the lake was going wild, dancing breakers slapping from all sides, and I realised the real-as danger, knew we really could capsize. We had been warned the water would be freezing and I could tell they had been scared for us, even as they sent us out here. They had given us life jackets which we wore concealed under our clothes, had assured us they were on standby to rescue us in this worst-case scenario. The local guy had said we wouldn't have much time.

I did as I had been directed, acted all calm, gazing this way then that at the frenzied water, all like this was some kind of normal for me—heart thundering inside of me loud as the giant black bug overhead, sodden hair lashing long whips into my face—see, I used the mirror of the lake's stillness way out beyond our radius of manmade mess, just kind of tuned into the same stillness which lived deep inside of me, gladdened I knew how to. The little boat tilted at some insane acute angle, the oars jolting and scraping, straining to free themselves from their anchoring loops. And gripping onto the sides, I saw the body of water open its gigantic toothless maw, tongue sucking right over our sinking edge, all hungry for us. My own body went nuts, electric-as, ready to run the nowhere it could; but my mind stayed achingly present, every detail magnified and almost too glorious, like every moment was a clear freeze frame in a movie. I felt every *thing* had a life. Icy water spat into my skin; and I knew and was inside every speck of it; I sensed this life as an expression of joy. I realised my body had softened inside, in an incredible sort of acceptance, felt myself interlinked with every particle of spit—and the blood of everything. The boat lurched and I was jolted backwards. It rolled, tipped the other way.

I saw how he just lay there below me, uncanny, a blonde kind of beardless Jesus, all like he was dead and the vessel was his tomb—and *oh no!* my mind grabbed a hold of me, telling me I might really die here—the searing water, the crazed look of it, seen now like a version of hell, giving me to know for sure I didn't want to die, like I sometimes thought I did, this way or any other. I took to silently begging for my life, gulping the wind to survive, as I placed myself back down onto him, my countenance cool-as, all pretending to go back to sleep. I realised he was mumbling away and I felt his body close to terror.

The helicopter veered off in a second. Just like that the water calmed. There was instant relief in my every cell, all like a switch had been flicked inside of me, and a sigh filled, splayed out in my body, released. The natural breeze went kind of warm, even though it wasn't, was left to roam all gentle, over our skins.

'Shit,' he murmured. 'Shit. Do you think we can move now?'

'I don't know. Didn't they say to wait?'

'For the signal, yep, they did. They can't see us though. Now the helicopter's gone.'

I felt him move his head and I tilted my own to catch his blue eye. 'But they can see the boat from the shore.' I opened and closed my palms, wiggled my stiff fingers. 'I'm freezing.'

He enclosed my hand in one of his own, firm and assured. 'You are. And you're soaking.'

'So are you,' I said.

'Oh...wow, yes, I am.' He was sliding his other hand about, feeling his clothing. And then a splish-splash sound. 'Shit, there's a lot of water in here. Are you okay? You're trembling.'

'Yeh. I thought we were going to flip right over.'

'So did I.'

'Did you look? Did you see the water?'

'No. I'm a pro, aren't I?'

'That was mental,' I said, feeling some kind of renegade laughter flare up inside of me, jerk through my body. It came spilling out and then he was laughing too and we were juddering against each other.

'You think they've forgotten us?' he crooned.

'Yes! The bastards.'

'Do they know what they put us through?'

'They have no idea. They just think we were rocking it up at some glamorous helicopter club, huh.'

'While they're taking bets on our lives. I can't believe they haven't checked in with us yet. To see if we're okay.'

'That's what they're doing—for sure—they're checking the video-playback.'

'The arseholes.'

'I wonder if they want to do another take—they said they probably would. I think I could do it better. I think I was maybe a bit too quick to lie down again.'

'I hope not.'

'I hope so.'

'You really are mad, you know that?'

A massive cold shiver quaked through me, on top of all the million trembles. 'No, I'm the pro.'

'Not so sure about that. More like you've got a death wish.'

A distant voice crackled out of nowhere. 'Okay guys—you're free to move. Can you hear me?'

He shot right up, flinging me with him, so I came up to sitting too. 'You know, I never heard the signal,' I told him. 'I just had to go for it.' He was fumbling as he extracted the walkie-talkie from where it was tucked into a waterproof bag down by his other side.

'Copy,' he said, all brute force.

'Copy,' I said under my breath, smirking.

'We're done on that shot. You can come in now.'

'Copy that.'

I snatched the radio, pressing the button with the side of my numb thumb. 'Hello? Hello, it's me.'

'Hello you.'

A tingling surge rose up from deep in my body. The way his voice went all sort of soft when he spoke to me, even through the harsh static. I felt almost warm all of a sudden, a new energy ripening in my chest. 'Was that okay? The timing I got up? I couldn't hear the cue, see. Aren't we going to do another one? I know I can do it better—now I know what happens.'

'You want to do another one?' His voice faded as he must have turned to the director or the producer maybe. 'She wants to do another one.' I couldn't hear what they were saying to each other as the radio hissed and sizzled. I made starry eyes at my co-star, who had gone all pinched, and he flashed me little switchblades.

Before he could say anything, I said, 'Copy.'

'This isn't funny.'

'Alright, Hutch.'

'I mean it. You said yourself we nearly went over.'

'What? You're too scared?'

'Well, no. If they want us to go again, of course I will.'

'But you'd rather not. You put yourself before the integrity of the work.'

'It's a cruddy pop video, for Christ's sake.'

'You've changed your tune. It's not cruddy. You said yourself it's a really cool song and we're lucky to be in this.'

'I do not particularly want to risk my life any more for something that doesn't matter.'

'What kind of attitude is that? Anyway, the record company's put a lot of money into this and you have no idea where this is going to—we might get to be a part of history.'

'We will *be* history, more like. If we die. And anyway, no one is going to make history from being in a pop—'

I laughed, made a "duh" kind of a face. '—I know. I know. I mean, you never know—I know. I just want to do a better take—'

The radio crackled in my hand as his voice came through '—sorry, guys, we've got it. It's a wrap on that scene.'

'But I know I can do it bet—'

'—pointless to argue, you. No negotiation on this one. I know you like to do your best job of it, and normally of course we'd go again. But it's been agreed, it's too dangerous this time.'

'Oh,' I said, my energy plummeting. I wanted to hurl the damn walkie-talkie into the lake. Scaredy-cat was staring at me, all triumphant.

'Cool with me,' he yelled out.

I shot him a taste of his switchblades, felt my mouth a tight little knot. 'He can't hear you.' I held up the heavy black oblong, its talk-button free-as. 'Duh.'

'Can you make your way in, please?' came the assistant-director's frazzled-up voice.

'Copy,' I said into the radio. And to my companion, I said, 'Get rowing.'

By the time we got to the shore, maybe half an hour later, and a couple of the crew were trotting into the shallows in their green wader wellie-things, me and ol' fearless were back on the friendly track with each other. We had gotten to laugh quite a bit, me bailing bathwater out of the boat with the pitiful tin cup they had given us as he rowed, the relief of life all spilling itself through us in some kind of essential way. The local safety dude and the whimp-arsed production assistant—who had weaselled his way next to me on the plane journey over, all snitching on what the messed-up zoned-out assistant director had been up to the night before, dirtying up his name—the two of them guided the pointed front of our dinghy through the black volcanic rocks, pulled it onto the dark sandish beach, as the wardrobe and make-up ladies came darting in, bearing coats and towels.

'My god, you're drenched right through,' wardrobe said to me, her hand squeezing at the sleeve of my jacket, so water trickled out. 'Come on, let's get you out of these. You too,' she called to ol' fearless, who was being fussed over by make-up, getting his head rubbed dry a few yards away.

She draped a huge pink towel around me, kind of yanked it tight, so I staggered about a bit, felt about five and like she was my mum and I had just been swimming in the baby pool. The life jacket felt like a rubber ring around me. 'Here,' she said, pushing the fat wedge of rolled-together edges into my claw beneath. I envisaged myself as a raw sausage as she indicated with her head toward the distant minibus parked on the sandy soil, tufty grasses sprouting all around it. Her arm came over my shoulders, driving me along with her. 'There's not much warmth in this sun—even though it's June—when *does* it get warm here, I'd like to know? We don't want you catching your death.'

'Everyone's obsessed with me dying,' I said.

'Well, they have good reason.' Her tone upped its anger, triggered my spine to shrink. 'That was dangerous—they compromised you. It was damn-well irresponsible, if you ask me. I'm not so sure they should have put you through that. I'm not even sure you'd be covered by the insurance.'

'It was fine,' I said. I wanted to tell her, Chill out, but I knew I would be pushing it and maybe making an enemy, so I zipped my mouth on that one. 'I'm fine. It was exciting. But how did it look? The shot? Did it work?'

'It worked,' she growled.

'So it looked like you didn't know why the water was suddenly going mental?'

'Hmm.' She was clearly reluctant to give any praise to the shot at all.

As we neared the minibus, I saw the small film crew a ways off, on an incline overlooking the lake, all silver and black boxes littering the landscape, helicopter on the beach below them, its blades in stillness, pilot standing next to it. The crew had just about finished packing away the equipment, while the director, the lighting-camera man, the producer and the assistant director were talking together in their cluster. I could see they still had the video-playback monitor up on a box and were maybe referring to it and I shrugged myself from under wardrobe's grip, let my sausage skin fall away, enjoyed the thudding softness of its undulating landing onto the dusty earth, all darting off toward them. Of course she called out, annoyance slicing through her pretty plea for my health and I yelled back I was fine and I would come in a minute (chill out).

I decelerated once I felt sufficiently away from her, took on an easy stride, spanning my vision to feast over the lake, which was all glassy, reflecting the sky and mountains and my inner stillness with unbelievable clarity and perfection. A kind of gorgeous sigh came up from deep within me, expanded that space of awe, some sort of greater knowing, in which along came my uncle all nodding his bald head and describing the energy of Love, he called it, which was bigger than all of this life. Trying not to feel the sting of how I missed him, rubbing him out from my mind as I had from my life, I took to imagining what the boat and my performance might have looked like from this vantage, picturing it through the camera where you wouldn't see the helicopter.

I stopped myself from sliding my sights back to the satellite group I was aiming for, but felt into them, into him in particular, and was gratified when my peripheral vision confirmed my feeling he was watching me. On a wild impulse, I pretended like I was heading right passed them, down to the lake. I paused and picked a kind of skinny-stemmed dandelion growing among the hollow beachy-type grasses my foot had kicked into, my body all a bit awkward on account of the life jacket.

'Hey,' he called, so I had to look at him. 'What're ya doing?' He beckoned me with his whole arm. 'Come and join us.'

I smiled, stuck the dandelion stem sideways between my lips, let my legs turn my trajectory, just spin on their own all under the gathered gypsy skirt they had decided on for my character. Something I would never wear myself. I felt acutely aware of its sodden fabric, all kind of cold and gluey, watering the ground every now and again, emptying itself, like I was some sort of specialised drying machine.

'Do you want to see the playback?' he asked me, as I drew near.

'Sure,' I said through the thread of flower stem, feeling its yellow head tickle my cheek all sweet and full of love.

'It's very good. You did well,' the director told me.

'That was pretty hairy,' his producer said, smiling, her eyebrows raised in appreciation. 'You really held it together—very impressive—we couldn't have asked for more under the circumstance.'

'Well, you could have,' I said. I pincered the dandelion stem between finger and thumb, twirled it in my fingertips as I dropped my hand. 'I really did want to do another take, you know. That just felt like a run-through to me, see. You didn't take full advantage.'

They all kind of laughed, giving me these looks that said I was young and naïve and maybe sweet and maybe funny. There came a tightness at my throat, a ghastly hot wave rising from my heart into my face.

'You really did miss the full potential,' I stated flat-as. I smiled, let my biting eyes flick into each of theirs, until I reached his. I was surprised when I just let them rest in him, allowing that dried-up-moss-looking green of his to penetrate me for a full moment. I felt a ping inside of me, a kind of delicious glory. I looked to the monitor, saying, 'Show me then.'

He ran the playback, and it looked brilliant, very enigmatic, but I was right, I had laid back down a lot too quick. There came a visceral disappointment in myself, some kind of anger I couldn't make it right.

The director said, as if in answer to what I didn't say, 'Yeh, you *were* a little quick—but that was natural under the circumstances—it must have been goddamn raw and overwhelming out there. And time would have abstracted, somewhat stretched for you, I mean, so it felt longer whilst it was happening, yes? but hold on—' he made an indication toward the monitor '—we shot it with two cameras—at different angles, you see—' another take began to play '—so we have more than enough footage to extend the moment. You see? *And* we have the helicopter shot from above—it's on super8, wasn't connected to playback, so we can't look at the rushes til later, but they're going to be great. I think you did a brilliant job.' He nudged me with his elbow, insisted with his eyes I look at him. 'Not many people could have handled that—and I'm sure *no* other seventeen-year-old girl could have achieved the convincing performance of serenity I needed, as you did. We got lucky with you, that's for sure.'

I slid my eyes away, stuck the dandelion stem between my front teeth this time, biting into its brittle end so I heard it crunch, tasted its bitter juice.

'Not lucky,' the AD said. 'I told you she had it in her, remember? After we made the Blabbermouth video. The way she handled that crazy shot, with the camera on the crane flying inches from her face. That was a fast action and this one didn't flinch.' He winked at me. 'I love that shot. You know, I'm also Rain's editor so I get very intimate with the footage.'

'I didn't know.'

'Yeah, I've been looking at you a—'

'—hey guys,' a voice called. It was the helicopter pilot, all beaming, his unfamiliar Icelandic accent catching a hold of my rude delight. 'I have room for one—back to the hotel. Anyone?'

'Yes, me,' I thrilled. 'I want to—'

At the same time, he: 'Yeah, I'm up for it.'

'—I'd love to—I've always wanted to go in a helicopter.' Realising he had expressed his own desire to go, I spun my eyes to his, all smiling, looked from the director to the producer and back to him. My body was electrified as he held me in his terrific smile, green eyes kind of moist and arresting. I was crazy for his thick curly lashes. It was obvious he liked me. Maybe it was *this* one who could ease my loss.

He gave me a nod, turned to the pilot. 'Great. Let's go, then.' To the rest of us, he said, 'Most excellent. See you back at the hotel.' And he was walking off, heading with the pilot toward the glittering beast on the black sands below.

Some Kind of Wild Rose and a Little Bit of Blue

The whole crew and everyone were sat to dinner along a long skinny table, formed, at the producer's behest, from several tables joined in a row. It had just kind of happened he was sitting opposite me. Or he had done it on purpose, I wasn't really sure. I had as much as possible been acting like he barely existed the last couple of days, and I didn't want to care where in hell he sat, but I did—I was springing with all kinds of jumpy-bumps he just didn't deserve.

It was our second-to-last night, was gossamer light out, even though it was close to midnight; I had discovered it was going to be light here forever this time of year and, five nights in, with hardly any sleep, I found I was never tired. We were up at five, on location and shooting by seven—scenes in stunning lunar-like landscape, in which ol' fearless had had to follow me about all over the place. My character was supposed to be a sort of spirit guide, not actually real—but you would only get to realise this at the end of the video, when I would disappear into the air, and it would explain all the weird phenomena happening around us, the suddenly crazed lake and everything. We had skirted spurting geysers and all the bubbling mud-stuff the country is famed for, plus we had done a kind of love scene in a sulphur pool deep within a cave, where we had to wear no tops to appear nude. Just us and a skeleton crew had had to crawl down a spikey-rocked tunnel to get there. The water had been warm and super-stinking of bad eggs, was said to be very good for you, full of minerals, made your skin soft-as, even though mine got pretty scratched up.

I was stroking my forearm quite a bit whilst he was yabbering on about some bigtime shoot or other he had worked on, for sure trying to impress me—when his foot came pushing really full against mine. The hairs at the back of my neck went static-as, prickling up, and straight away waves came rippling through me—his foot still pushing—and I was for sure expanding way beyond my body, all sort of falling *up!* into the sky—his foot pushing away and—*oh!* my spirit didn't waste any time, I felt myself the stars, the moon, even the sun on the other side of the world, shining all over Australia—so I knew myself as innocent again, just tender thirteen, in that bed at my friend's house with mean ol' robi

me and robin remi

my energy gone all nuts in ways I had never known existed, just with playing footsi

am crazy for hi

{footsi}es. And now I was sure this one's foot was pressing even harder into mine. I stared into him, wondering, Was he doing it deliberately? He gave me no sure signal, just eyeballed me as he carried on with his show-offy story. His foot made little twists and scuffs, the fuzz of his leg-hair grazing my bare shin—and my skin answered, went all tight right up past the scalloped hem of my Sixties suede mini-skirt, heat like fingers all nestling into the rude pink flower of me. He made contact with my other foot, fired up that starkly present oblivion of my first ever turn-on—*oh yes!* it was just as delectable; badly, badly delectable—and for a crazy second my heart cried for Robin Remick, like I was still that kid of then. But Robin Remick meant nothing to me anymore—*more*—I hated him now. He wasn't the one.

I threw myself into the eyes of the assistant director, let him stream into me, my breath all ragged and high in my chest—until with a kind of slap, I saw what I was up to, yanked myself back to reality: I didn't want to give myself to *this* him either—was I nuts? My body almost hurt. This him wasn't the one, of course he wasn't the one, and he never could b

walking down the hentrack pathway under the bluest sky *him* the smell of his sweat reaches for me wraps me big square fingers they hold me his kisses blur me into the earth they suck me out of myself i am all lip i am nothing and everythi

{never could b}e, just impossible, no one could because *he* had that place and always would. My longing for my real him opened up cracks inside of me, I felt them widening, all breaking me, and I knew I had to stop this before I fell apart. Already the quakes were coming. Already, my eyes burni

i see my reflection in the blue of his eyes in the black of the pupil a tiny me made knowable through hi

{burni}ng. *Stop,* I said to myself. *Please stop.* I just about sprung up, saw in my mind's eye my chair flung backward, clattering behind me, heard my terrible sobs over the scrambling shambles of my footsteps, a commotion all rising from the table as I fle

running down the hentrack pathwa

d. But somehow I steadied myself. I stayed. Gave myself into the

mossy eyes opposite me, saw he was into me, for sure he was into m
runni dow the he

e. I pressed my foot into his, leaned forward on my elbows, all cupping my face, smiled so my tear-glossed greys would come over as some sort of ecstatic bliss. 'Pour me some more of that fancy vodka,' I said, light as air. 'All that lava-filtered artic waters crap tastes pretty good, huh?' Our knees glanced, feet shifted right up against each other, all like it might be incidental.

He leaned his lean body across the length of the table to grab a hold of the bottle, his leg all pushing into mine. He had to stand a little and I saw his flesh, the hint of light hair growing out of his shorts at the groin-line, as his t-shirt rose. He wore funny kinds of clothes that were always too small for him, always his wrists sticking quite a bit beyond his Harrington jacket cuffs, and I found it somehow compelling, this boyish quality in an older man, like no one I had known before. I had clocked his slice of torso many a time, when hanging around waiting as they set up a shot. He sloshed several fingers of vodka into both our glasses.

'Do you want a mixer?' he asked me, already reaching for another bottle. 'You were having tonic, right?'

'No thanks.'

He raised his eyebrows, grinned, and I realised the gap between his small front teeth wasn't a gap at all, but a stain. 'Ice?'

I shrugged. I would've drunk it just like that but I liked making him work for me. 'A couple of pieces.' He did my bidding, asking someone to pass the ice bucket, lengthening himself again to get it from them. I wondered how old he was. In his twenties for sure, mid-twenties—a few years older than my flatmate I reckoned.

I swirled my ice into my drink, enjoying its delicate music. I took a large mouthful, held it a moment, tasting the smooth lemony flavour, let it slide down my throat to a peppery burning finish. I nodded. 'It's good stuff. Maybe we should take some home?'

He nodded in return—the elevated eyebrows, the stain again—that nasty stain causing strange whispers inside of me. He asked where I lived, and we bantered around about bits of our lives, laughing a lot, all that footsie-legsie-playtime lark, enriched by the high of the flowing alcohol, keeping me hooked and buzzing. He told me he lived in a squat, and I nodded in vague recognition, choosing not to tell him I knew all about that life, didn't want to dirty anything about the splendour I had lived when I was fifteen. He let me know he didn't have a girlfriend. 'Haven't had one in over a year,' he qualified, without me asking. He winked. I hated it when men winked. 'But I'm not a saint.'

'You don't say?' I said.

'Oh?'

I shrugged. 'I got your picture.'

He seemed to like that. I let the delectable wavy feelings recharge, make fresh raw floods at each subtly placed foot and shove, let the yearning bloat and pop, so I felt all vast and out-of-bodied again, whilst satisfied I was in control.

The dinner table broke up, reminders from the production assistant idiot we were up at five tomorrow for our last day's shoot. 'Time for your beauty sleep,' he told me, in that slimy kind of a way he had. He shot the AD a terse look, obliging us to take ourselves to our beds along with everyone else. Our rooms were right next to each other, like fate kept pushing us together, and we journeyed side by side up the corridors, all kind of swaying, our shoulders bumping, my insides shooting glitter-bombs. My heart was fast as we said goodnight outside our doors. I fixed my eyes to his, waiting for him to invite me into his room, taken aback when he made no move, my excitement, that illusive mantle of happiness, slipping away to expose some sort of dark perplexity as I enclosed myself within my own room.

I kicked off my sandals, sat on the edge of my narrow bed, mind going into the kind of overdrive my uncle had taught me the Buddha qualified as self-made suffering—false, clinging, just story, all that rubbish. I felt shards of rage at my uncle, was appeased, in all the surging pain, by my vengeful refusal still, to let him back into my life. But his voice came running through me like a banshee, rose up out of me and into the eerie shadows of the night-time daylight, telling me, in a disembodied slurred-up whisper: 'Be here now—this now—be you with You. Just simple pure energy.'

I was sickened to hear myself; that tingling energy he would guide me into igniting in my hands, brightening in my head; but I was sort of gladdened too—owned I missed him—hated him for it—loved him in the hate, all understanding stuff we had talked about way-back-when with an unexpected burning clarity. Love and hate were a part of a whole, just like he had said; they were locked together, light and shadow, beauty and pain; the hate there to show you love was the true; I got it.

I realised thick hot tears were hitting my hands. Enough, I said to myself. Enough tears you have shed. And my uncle piped up, You have the choice, my lovely, you have dominion over yourself. You are Awareness. Witness yourself, this moment, in kindness—for this too shall pass.

But I *didn't* have a choice. Agony just spewed up from inside of me. I was wishing I could go back to heather-hazed Ireland—while I was stuck in volcanic Iceland—would I ever be Angel Face to my Swan Neck again? And where was he anyway? Now? I nearly wanted to kill my uncle.

Catapulting from the bed, I staggered into the neat hotel bathroom, plunged my face into a fluffy white towel, expelled my howl there, a hot-breathed return coming to suffocate me. I found myself wishing for death again. But I couldn't keep my body from lurching itself out of the grip of the towel. I saw a comic book Joker-face imprinted on the terry cloth from all the makeup I hadn't removed after shooting. I looked up into the mirror, saw the real Joker, all smudges of grief, some kind of ghostly enigma of primal emotion giving shine.

On a crazed impulse I snatched up a sandal from the oatmeal carpet of the bedroom, propelled myself, knees-first, onto the bed, drove its sole fast into the party wall, so it made a sharp smack. I did this again, all relishing the echo. I held my breath, listened, a lush sort of messed-up elation licking onto my lips. My heart was going like church bells, way up in my belfry. I slapped at the wall several more times, stood from the bed, stayed kind of hunched as my ears reached for a sign of his reply. Blinking rapidly, I found myself sashaying back into the bathroom. Fuck him, I said to myself. I'll fucking show him. I wetted a corner of the towel under the tap, slid its rough surface under and around my eyes, cleaned the streaks from my cheeks, wiped it over my torn-looking lips, into which I smeared some minty lipbalm.

I went out into the corridor, stood outside his room. I waited. My nerves like spaghetti boiling in my belly. I slapped aside all kinds of shadows that pressed at me. I knocked. Waited. There came the soft sounds of movement from within. And the handle was moving downwards, the door drawn inwards—and there he was, with his white duvet all wrapping him, almost girly, the way it was tucked under his arms, those long limbs showing their tender hairless uppers into elegant clavicle and shoulders. He looked surprised, unsure for a moment, then registered the full implication of my being there. He grin came with its slice of stain, which looked like a gap again.

'Hello you.'

'Hi.'

'Are you alright?'

'Mmmm.'

We just stood gazing into one another for a delicious gut-snagged eternity. He reached one lean arm and took a hold of my hand. There were lovely hairs on his forearms. He drew me into him, all soft sway, stepped back to close the door. His smile grew, kind of like a child's, small-toothed, wide-mouthed and...I don't know...sort of awed...and sort of like he was chewing on gum in that exaggerated way kids do in pleasure. I heard a click inside his cheek. His hand came and curled itself round my face as his mossy eyes held me. And we were leaning in and we were kissing and all my pent-up feeling was releasing, an unbound freedom letting me live again, spiralling through me so I was soaring and expansive and tuned to my potential; I went all merged with the milky light in the room, with the landscape beyond, with this him and *that* him, somehow made whole, a part of the whole, my body tingling in wild wide arcs, outward and inward at once, the dense ache of my wanting coming as pleasure in the pain. He was taller than me, so my head tilted up to reach him. I pushed him up against the veneered cupboards of the narrow corridor which opened into the room, a room exactly like mine, the bathroom an echo of my recent explosion, gleaming white, behind me. The kiss was a whole-body kiss. Our lips and tongues were swollen and in harmony—I couldn't believe the extent of the high, some kind of physical chemistry I had only ever known with one other, with *him*, like our bodies might be made for each other—I couldn't believe another body could ever be made for mine—and somehow I let the idea flood me, aware I was flooding the confines I had set myself. My body was flooding. I could feel the wet coming out of me, out of the opening wild rose that dwelt between my legs.

He broke the kiss to draw me around the shallow corner, pulled me with him and his duvet, which he released as we fell onto the slender bed. He wore dotted boxer shorts, white on black, and as I lay myself over his slim and fine-looking form, I felt his cock pressing against me, the nature of me responding, all pushing my hips into him in answer, these sweet and urgent noises escaping us unbidden. He flipped me onto my back, reached down, indulged in the snap of each of the poppers down the front of my suede mini-skirt as they released. Tugged off my t-shirt so we thrilled as our skins made soft warm contact for the first time.

Time disappeared. We got naked, rolled and tumbled, slid up and slid down each other, tasted and knew the body of the other. We shared ourselves, all kinds of explosions shuddering and juddering through us until we lay quiet, my head on his shoulder, arms about each other, breath gone soft.

I was drifting somewhere joyful, abstract, when he jostled me. There might have been a blanket of tiny blue flowers, all open-petaled and crushed beneath my knees. Maybe.

'Hey...' he said, voice far away.

'Hmmm?'

'Where's your little flower?'

'What—you wha...? Flowers? How—?'

'Your little flower?'

'Oh...' I felt the froth of a giggle at my throat, nestled my face into his neck. 'My flower? You know where my *flower* is.'

'I do.' He pressed a finger into the delicate groove where my petals split, to show me. I felt delicious tuggings at my darling bud, felt myself jolt inside, kept this for myself. 'But the dandelion you had in your mouth, after the lake, you little pretty?'

'What dandelio—oh, *that* flower... The dandelion? I don't know. I dropped it. What makes you think of that dandelion?'

He shrugged, I felt it, then sat up a little, so I had to rise up too, all half there, on my elbow, as he reached for something on his sidetable—a paperback. He held it up so I could see the title. It was *A Clockwork Orange*. 'Do you know this?'

'Good book,' I said.

'Genius,' he said. He fanned through the pages until they fell open. He showed me the open 'V'. And I saw he had the dandelion there, all dried now, its stem bent up in a few places, so it looked skeletal.

'You've got it?'

'I found it—in the minibus.'

'Oh. But why did you keep it?'

'Because it had been in your mouth. Where I wanted to be.' He touched his bald forefinger into my lip. I had seen how he was biting his nails all the time, when he was concentrating whilst working. Bitten as far as was possible, they were, so his fingers popped out like crazy erections. 'You sexy little thing, you.'

I paused, felt suddenly quite awake, my stomach gone cold. 'But you went off in the helicopt

        running down the hentrack pathw

er...'

'I only found it yesterday.'

'Oh. Oka

        big square fing

y...'

'You don't like that I have your flower?'

I nodded, averted my eyes. 'I li

        beautiful blue flowers all crushe

ke.'

'I've been wanting this,' he said. He took my hand, kissed my knuckles, kind of made me look at him, his mossies all into me. 'I've been wanting to do this for ages.'

'Have you?'

'I didn't imagine I would get the chance.'

I nodded, smiled. 'Lucky you, then, huh?'

Blue Speedwell

The dense song of a mass of violins was cascading full-on out of my flatmate's room and into mine, all ecstatic melancholy entering my body, the strings vibrating inside of my every cell, sort of forcing them bigger it felt like. I took a hold of the hem of my massive t-shirt, on a reflex reading its STAY ALIVE IN 85 all backwards in the speckledy mirror of my wardrobe, the moment before I tore it over my head. And then I just stood there, all nearly nude, just not getting ready, the t-shirt hanging from one hand—it was all I could do, with the skyward spiralling harmonies thickening, blurring. I leaned in, stared into my eyes close-up, found myself as someone else staring into them; I was he, gazing into me. Palest blue heaven into cloud
          am thrown wide ope
y grey. His eyes came as some kind of hell, even as they were certain rapture. I wanted to be with him; it was a place in me I couldn't stand or shed—nor wanted to. I found myself moving from

my room, t-shirt dragging, feet all kind of skating over the old floorboar

        grass soft and prickly beneath he hard within me he soft and prickly above his stubble shears the skin of my fa

{floorboar}ds of the living room, all through the electric light, just about conscious, coming to lean my shoulder on her doorjamb. The doorjamb felt good. It felt solid. It said somehow, *I'm holding you.* Just as the floorboards had. These things contained me and let me be this disembodied someone, floating elsewh

        is lying beneath me i rise up into the soft summer ai

{elsewh}ere, whilst being stark-as there. I watched Jessie all involved, hunched on the floor, her farmgirl's fing

        up! into the blue shimmeri

{fing}ers working the scissors, turning a photograph as the blades went around a figure. I felt a surge of love for her. She had a funny way of working her jaw on each cut, like she was cutting with her whole bei

        crushing the tiny blue flowe

{whole bei}ng. She caused me to come present to the love I felt for her. I saw she was constructing a new collage, layering images with tiny found objects, with metal washers and string and copper wire, the way she did. A mess of off-cuts was scattered all about her, seeming to spin and drift to the music. The violins came into their swirling overlapping climax, the deep singular base note of the cello keeping its constant hum beneath, all like an out-breath that never ceased. Jessie looked up, saw me, not a moment's fright. Her eyes hooked to mine, and I knew she knew, and I saw she just let *me*; her gaze all golden-syrup, purer than that, just gold, a lioness watching over her cu

        i see my reflection in the blue of his eyes in the black of

the pupi

{her cu}b. As the music ended, a bell completing its painful beauty, the dense residue of sound played out its vibration so you could hear it long after it faded, like maybe that sound never actually stopped and kind of rung out over layers and layers of every sound and thought and word and went on for days and years and all eterni

flecks of my blood in the tender-blue flowe

{eterni}ty. The silence was punctuated by the needle snapping a rhythm on the black vinyl record. I felt how she and I were breathing in tandem, the rise and fall of us gentle-as.

'Hey,' she said, patting the floor next to her.

I took myself over, dropped as I was, just in my pink flower-print knickers, onto my bottom beside her. She encircled me in her arms. I felt like I was a part of her collag

blue flowers of the speedwe

{part of her collag}e. Her linen smock was sweet-scented, kind of scratchy against my naked skin. Drawing herself away, she pinched my chin between finger and thumb, all smiling and radiant.

'Please come,' I said. 'You know you want to, see.'

'Ahhh.' It was a pleasured sigh. 'I'm having such fun, my lil' darlface…'

I wrinkled my nose. 'I know you don't want to. I know. Maybe I'll stay too.'

She shook her head, her shorn fair hair catching glints in the strong light she used. 'No. You want to go. Come on now. Merl and Todd-baby will be here soon to fetch you. And they are well excited.' She took a hold of her glue pot, a kind of wallpaper-type paste, stirred the stumpy-bristled brush about in it, laid it back down on her other side as she levered herself up to standing. 'A little spliffy? I've got a new batch of home-grown just dried, lovely and mellow. Go on, go and finish dressing. I'll make one up. The boys are going to like that methinks.'

As if they heard her, the bell rang out. We giggled.

'Don't let Merl see you like that or he'll be wanting to film you. I guarantee. And then Todd-baby's going to get in a grump waiting.'

I nodded, all laughing, piped, 'Put some music on,' went scarpering across the sitting room and into my bedroom, enjoying the feel of my long legs all skittish like a young racehorse. In that moment I simply felt the joy of the horses and the blue flowers and *him* inside of me, the loss somehow coming as a tasty residue, like a dab of sherbet fizzing on my tongue. The slam of my door was like a fantastic full-stop, after which came a colossal paragraph of booming reggae. I yanked myself into the cherry-red cat suit our adored Lauren had cut the neck out of and given to me a couple of years back, that first time I had had the guts to go clubbing with the gang of them all. I could feel the sweetness of myself back then, right in the fibres of the stretchy cotton fabric, youth and naivety all caught up in the mix of my then radical grown-up knowing. I stepped into my designer denim frill, as Lauren had christened it, a tiny skirt with sort of integrated knickers, something she had borrowed back then, for styling on a shoot, and gotten away with not returning, determined on my keeping it because "it works like it's been made for you, girlfriend", all in her New York drawl, her black skin glowy-as. It was my surprise to her I was wearing the look she'd put together then—she always gave the most satisfying response to one of her old outfits making an unexpected show.

There came the buzz of our friends entering, yelled hellos, shoes on wood. The scuffing and crazed high-pitched singing-along to Jimmy Cliff—Todd-baby straight into dancing as usual. My door flew open, Merl in its wake, all dark brown hair, brown eyes, brown skin, already his Bolex 16mm camera up to his eye, and I did a little dance myself, before telling him to quit it and grabbing a hold of him so the camera got wedged between us, all digging into me. I felt him release the shutter, drop his arm, let it hang as he hugged me.

'Just lie down on the bed a mo for me, would you?' His Edinburgh burr came like whispered cigarette smoke. 'Just for one quick shot.' I eyed his styled-up Sixties electric-blue trackpants, the way he wore them almost hanging off, the dense cotton pulled out at the thighs, jodhpur-like, with his long-looking exaggerated brogues and his immaculate kiddish cow's-lick, courtesy of Todd-baby.

'Good look,' I said.

'One quick shot.'

'Yes, maestro,' I echoed his accent, diving onto my bed. 'But let's not annoy Todd-baby tonight.'

'He's okay—he's getting his spliff, eh?' He attended to my position. 'Okay, open your arms wide—and up a bit—yeh, make a kind of arc, so your arms are like a ballerina's Swan Lake type wings. Yes! That's it. Great. I like the way you're holding your hands—you've really got the vibe. You're a kind of angel, you get me?' I nodded. 'Okay, so I'm going to start on a wide, then pan up your body as I come in, and end on a mega-boom close-up of your angel face.'

'Angel Fa

        angel fac

ce?'

'Aw. Shite. I'm sor

        my reflection in the blue of his ey

ry.'

'It's okay. It's oka

        in the black of his pupi

y.'

'Hey shit, your eyes are all welling up. Can we just go for it? I want to catch this. Can you? Is that alright? Do you mind?'

'Go on,' I said quickly. 'Might as well honour the moment.' The Swan and the Angel, I wanted to sa

       a tiny me made knowable through hi

y. 'Go on, quick then.'

'Fab. You *are* an angel—you just are. Or shouldn't I say that?'

I smiled, small pricklings biting at my gut. 'You always have—haven't you? But maybe leave off of the face bit, yeh?'

'Got'cha. Right, I'm going for it—ready?' But he paused, camera up by his face. His voice came soft-as, 'Hey, but you sure you're alright to do this now? After all? I don't want to be taking advantage in a bad kind of a way, eh.'

'Yup. Yes, I want to.'

'Thank you. You're the best, you know that? It's going to look sensational. Ready then? Ah yeh, and I'll cue you for a smile—no teeth—through those wet gleamers—can you? And—*action*.'

We did the shot just the once, and when he came to my close-up I let a few tears out too, as some kind of weirdo bonus, to mark my love, and then the lippy smile all just like he wanted. He told me he had some feathery white wings for me to wear at the club, said he liked the way I didn't have on a jot of makeup, it was going to be perfect for his film.

And then we were waving our goodbyes to Jessie, and Merl was driving us up All Saints Road, up to Notting Hill Gate, alongside the green flashes of Kensington Gardens and its inner roadway beyond the fence, passing Marble Arch, and all the way into town.

We parked on Soho Square, came down Greek Street in our tight little crew. Todd-baby wore his honey-blonde hair in two plaits coming out of a pork pie hat, had on thick black eyeliner and dark lipstick, making his blue eyes bluer, his thin lips thinner. His jacket was a twist on something Victorian, structured, short-waisted, the crook-shaped sleeve configured to fall below the shoulder line. Merl, fingers all interlaced with his, bounced at his side, his cow's-lick living it large, camera bag strapped across his chest; whilst me, I kicked along in my Portobello Market-found hobnail boots, soon to dance, all buoyed-up in cat suit and denim frill, giant angel wings flapping at my back.

The thud of the bass came like an appetiser as we strode right up to the front of the queue, wrestled our way through the flamboyant cluster at the entrance, to be granted right of way the moment the cool black bouncer in his MA-1 jacket saw us. It was as if he were Jesus parting the red sea. The wild be-wigged cashier waved us in for free, high Hellos, How are yous, bouncing about the narrow lobby through the ever-increasing volume of our soundtrack.

We hit the interior, the music now ear-splitting, a glorious assault smacking every sense: vivacious colours, patterns, lycra, leggings, stockings, massive wigs, hats—someone wearing lit light-bulbs sprouting from his jacket—heels for days, white skin, black skin, brown, men as women, girls as boys all denim-ed up—you couldn't tell at a glance male from female, and even at a closer look, some were indefinable—both or neither—it didn't matter—makeup and hair like you never saw, on both genders; the heady mix of a million perfumes, of the thick fog of cigarettes and alcohol, so you tasted it, all like some sort of brash alien air; and the heat, the sweat, the wet skin you slipped against with any naked part of your own slicked skin as you bumped about in the crowd. It was incredible. The dancing: weird, playful, serious, singular, alive. And shared. All kinds of performances, each their own. Equality. Bliss. Freedom.

I danced on just fizzy water, Lauren finding me, all saluting me in the outfit she'd put together a couple of years before, delight spilling through her cool as she took to bopping opposite me energetic-as, her curvaceous body clothed in a frayed denim mini-skirt and a magnificent balloon-sleeved shirt, hair all bleached these days and still ironed, as she liked to say. Merl went about filming everyone, adding to his archive, from which he was making a new film.

We partied all the way up to the rude finish, to the moment of seeming-silence, just shrieks and calls, once the thud and scream of the music snapped shut. The disco lights went lurid strip, highlighting all—the smeared floor, the sweating walls, our garish soggy selves.

Merl grabbed a hold of my hand. 'Come on, angel, let's get you home.'

'Home-schmoome,' Lauren drawled. 'Party at yours?' she said, eyes flitting from Merl to Todd-baby.

'Yeah,' I said.

'Sure thing,' said Todd-baby.

Merl laughed, fingers lacing into mine. 'Of course—like, duh, huh?'

We made our way through the slowly thinning bedlam. There were goodbyes and kisses, high-fives and see-yas, along with a few invites, all the way out into the crisp fresh air of dawn-splashed London.

'I'm starving,' I said.

'You are *not* kidding,' Lauren said.

'For deffo,' chimed Todd-baby. To Merl, he said, 'Edgware Road? Falafel and chips?'

'Oh yeah,' I said, as Merl nodded. 'And fresh carrot juice, huh?'

There came a chorus of agreement from the other friends we had picked up along the way, arrangements of how we would all get there, more see-yas, and the legging it, elated-as, back to the car, me, Merl and Todd-baby all kind of as one being, linked also into Lauren and her fabulous dancer-choreographer friend I sometimes got to work with for fashion shows—and even on one of Merl's films one time—all of us for sure linked together by the finest threads of gold, like from our hearts and inner nature it felt.

Butterfly Bush

I woke super-early, not even six, the July sun shoving its sure fat body through the gaps around my blind, all impatient to get a look at me. I tried to go back to sleep but it didn't take long before I decided to get up, whizz my blind around its roller, invite the sun to just slosh right in as I trotted off in my big ol' STAY ALIVE t-shirt, to make myself a tea. I chose an Earl Grey, still took it black, always a resonance of him in tha

        he took a sip of my black tea; black like his, but mi

t. I realised I was humming as I brought my cup back to bed, propped myself up with my fluffed-up pillow, then went what looked like quiet, to the sunshine, or some imaginary watcher, say, or maybe just me looking in on myself from the outside, my mind getting busy-as, going over the lines of my speech in a fast kind of way all inside my head. I still was going to rehearse it full-out a couple of times

33

before I went off, but I would do this later, after my shower. I had loads of time—extra loads now.

There came a light tapping at my door, Jessie poking herself through the gap she produced, her own milky brew all leading her, steam filaments splitting around her smiley visage. 'Good morning, darl.'

'Yes,' I said, cuffing the space next to me. 'C'mon.'

She passed me her tea, had to crawl up the bed, which was rammed into the corner, and once she was settled next to me with my other pillow up her back, I returned her cup into her hands.

We just held each other's eye, all kind of sweet and full of everything we knew and shared. Then we gazed out the Victorian sash window, squinting through the ripe sunlight at the yellow-bricked Fifties council block across the street—bits of London that hadn't made it during the war—and up at the searing blue above it. I let my mind go still for real this time. We slurped on our hot tea, drawing air through it as it sucked into our mouths.

'Are you excited?' she said, after a while.

'I don't know…'

'I heard you humming. You seem very relaxed about it.'

'Yeh… Yes. Do you know? I kind of am—excited. You're right. But I'm not too much thinking about it. Will you watch my speech again before I go?'

'Of course. *I'm* excited. I know it's going to go brilliantly and they'll give you a place. They'll be lucky to have you.'

We smiled together some more. Chatted about this and that, the way you do, until something snuck up and snagged at a thought I had sort of hidden way-deep inside of me. But not very well. I went silent for a long noisy moment.

'He still hasn't called,' I said, my voice coming all croaky. 'It's weird, huh?'

'Yeah. It's making me not like him, for sure.'

'It's been nearly two weeks.'

'I know.

'He said a week.'

'I know.'

'He was away on that shoot for a *week*.'

She nodded, musing. She shrugged, mouth pulled down. 'Maybe they had to extend for some reason…it happens…but even so, he still could call you, no excuse—even from Cuba—I mean they have phones in Cuba—no doubt in his hotel room. Darlface. I'm so soz…'

'You think maybe something's happened to him?'

'Well—I don't know. I doubt it. Someone would surely call you for him—if it had. God, it's so frustrating you can't just call him. I mean, who hasn't got a telephone these days?'

'It's because it's a squat.'

'I know. But, hey, even we had one, didn't we?'

'But it was a payphone. How did we get a *payphone*?'

She made a wry kind of face, lips sucked in. 'In fairness, it was already there.'

I smiled, remembering the heavy Bakelite receiver. 'It was kind of old, huh? Funny someone put in a payphone in their own house.'

'It must have been shared, before us, huh? That happened a lot in the Seventies—in the Sixties—god, in the Fifties too…it was a huge house…'

I gazed into my empty mug where it lay between my hands on my lap. There were abstract reflections in the tea-shined bottom. A shard grated in my throat, split my voice when I spoke. 'What if he died? They wouldn't call me because they don't know me. None of his friends knows me.'

'Hey...' her voice came soft, made me look at her, eyes askance, all of a sudden feeling like I might just cry. 'Oh my little darlface...that's so unlikely. And the production company know you—they know you're seeing each other, don't they, you said? He made a thing of it on the journey home—in the minibus and the plane and everything. And didn't you go see him at the edit? And at that party you hated, at the producer's house, no? They know you. He hasn't died.'

'I know. I guess I may as well accept he just doesn't want to see me after all.'

A tender smile puffed through her nose, and I could see she felt for me. She looped her little finger around mine. 'Maybe...yeah, that's probably best.'

'He wasn't so nice, anyway.'

'What a dick.'

'I should've known.'

'Yeah...what a write-off.'

'Yeh, a write-off—that's what I have to do: write him off.' I made a sharp nod. 'A stupid collision, that's all it was. I never liked him much anyway. I know what love is and I didn't love him—not really. Just for some reason, I couldn't stop thinking about him—he's there somewhere, in some coil in my brain, even when I think he isn't. But I will. I'll stop.' I heaved a big breath, let it out all in a rush of sound, clonked my teacup onto my bedside table, flipped back the blankets. I stood, gave my friend another of those tight little nods, lips all tucked into themselves. 'Right. I'm going for my shower. I'm going to clear my mind and get ready. More important things to think about than a stupid man.'

Taking myself through the gate of the old red brick Primary school, a rash of nerves came spreading through my belly, surprised me in a way I didn't like and I had to remind myself nerves were kind of a good thing for a performance—if you knew how to use them. Just like with the racehorses once they were trained to understand.

They asked me for my name, checked a list, ticked me off, and I let my attention flutter up into the purple tails of a buddleia bush growing out of the wall above their heads, feeling myself a butterfly all lured by its lovely scent. Then I was being ushered down a side ally and directed into a dark hallway, old parquet flooring all echoing underfoot.

'Are you a student?' I asked the curly blonde girl escorting me.

'Yes. They think it's helpful and friendly to give prospective students a chance to meet those of us who already study here. Have you got any questions?'

'Um...not really. Do you like it here?'

She nodded, her eyes closing, mouth pulled in, like maybe she wasn't sure. 'Yeah. It's the best.' Her eyes went wide and all staring at me when she added, 'It's tough, though.'

'Tough?'

'The Method. They really put you through stuff here—no mucking about. It's not for everyone. But *anyway*...' She indicated a row of wooden chairs against one side of the hallway. A couple of people were already waiting there, and they each caught my eye, smiled, all probably shitting themselves, trying to look cool. 'Take a pew. I'll come and get you when they're ready for you.'

As it transpired, I was the second one called in. The waiting lad was from out of London, Canterbury or Coventry—or was it Canada?—I couldn't remember the moment he said it, like my brain went AWOL every time he spoke—but the gist was, he was hours early and had already sat there forever, watching people going in and coming out. I saw terror in his eyes when he started to say how most of them "got out" looking pretty shaken up, and I cut him off, told him, 'You could just go wander about for a bit. Go to a café or find a little park or something—you know, London is famed for its parks—there's always something.' But he declined, said he might get lost, even though he still had a couple of hours to go and I saw he had a London *A-Z*, just like I did, for getting about. Someone else arrived then, sat down between us, and I took out the play I was auditioning from, put my nose down, focused into my character preparation.

My curly friend presented me to the panel of people behind a long put-together table, six or seven of them maybe, and I was directed to set up my scene on the raised stage in front of them. I drew a chair into the centre—next to it, a small round table—extracted a mug and a packet of sweets from my bag. I had come in my chosen outfit, for which I had gone charity shopping—a mid-calf grey pleated skirt and a little chequered shirt, over which I slipped a frilly apron. They told me to begin when I was ready, so I took a long pause, centred myself—and then I was doing it and time seemed swallowed up—because then it was done.

There followed silence. The sifting of papers. Bodies shifting.

'So,' boomed a voice. 'You think acting is about emotions?'

My eyes skimmed the row of faces, landed on the speaker in the centre. He was clearly very tall, quite wiry, the planes of his face shaved to sharp angles. I saw he wore a mocking kind of a smile, eyes all squinty. He looked like a caricature, sort of like Punch, and like he might have a truncheon under the table.

I gave a soft smile. 'At its heart, yes.'

His face went to the side, cagey, crow-like. 'Ah. And beyond that?'

'Well...' I sat back down in my chair. 'Yes: emotion first, and then obviously presence—and voice—I mean articulation of voice, right, particularly for theatre—physicality—charac—'

'—you think you have heart, then?'

I gazed down at him from my perch. 'Yes. I mean, I actually do. I have heart.'

He slowly nodded, right down to his waist. 'Good. You do.' He looked like he wanted to break it. 'And why do you want to act?'

'Really?' I said.

'Excuse me?'

'I mean, is that a question?'

The room went taut, sort of like a tightrope was forming for me.

'This isn't a rehearsal, you know,' he said.

'Oh. I mean, I kind of thought...well, you wouldn't expect me to be perfect...would you? Otherwise I wouldn't need to be here to learn and be directed for the real thing. I want to learn to use my voice, see—and my body, for further expression.'

'This is your interview. It *is* the real thing.'

'Oh yes—of course. My interview—I get you. And yours too. In a way, see. Don't you think?'

'There are a lot of people that want to come here, people who would give their right arm for it.'

'Yup, and I would like to come here too. I think. Or I thought so anyway.'

'Have you any experience in acting?'

I gave that sharp nod I had been cultivating since the morning. 'Some. I've done quite a few videos, some adverts and a lot of art films.'

'No theatre?'

'Not yet. Apart from one time, in a club.'

'In a club? What sort of club?'

'You know—a *club*—like what was called a disco or a dancehall or whatever. It was up on a proper stage, like this one, only bigger—at that massive place in Charing Cross that used to be a theatre, see.'

He did his whole-body nod again, slow-as. 'My advice to you is to go get some experience and come back next year. How old are you?'

'Seventeen. It's on my application. I have experience, I told you.'

'Videos—*pop* videos, do you mean?—and adverts are not experience. And you're very young. Take your time. You have plenty of it.'

'Sure.' I said. I wanted to say, You old fart.

I rose from the chair, gathered up my sweet wrappers into my mug. I didn't know if I was angry or mirthful or gutted. I wanted to do the speech again. I wanted to say, Why don't you give me direction? See how I can grow? See how responsive I am? Try me? I nearly did too. I knew I could impress them. I knew it, because it happened all the time, when I worked with directors and I gave them every nuance of what they wanted—and more. And what about the films? I wanted to yell. You left those out conveniently. You didn't even ask about them.

I went all easy down the steps at the side of the stage, doublebacked to the table, stood right up in front of him. I took a leaf out of his mean-man's book, and, milking my moment, perused all the faces looking back at me before I said anything; they let me too. 'What's the point of coming to drama school if you go off and do it all already?' I said. 'This is where I would learn theatre and voice training the best. Isn't it? I'm ready to commit. I know what I want and why I want it and I'll do this with or without you.'

'Very good,' he said. 'Bravo.'

A woman with long wavy brown hair and a tiny button nose leaned into my eyeline. I noticed she stayed him with her hand on his forearm. And I saw him tense. 'I liked your work. We wouldn't normally say this, you understand. We have yet to make our decision. You'll be notified by post.'

I felt my eyes get smarty as I held her gaze. I realised she was warning me, telling me to take it easy and not blow my chances.

'I like your spirit,' old Punch said. 'Do as I say and come back next year.'

And what? I felt like saying. You'll tame me? As I cast my eyes down, a stupid tear fell, met its death somewhere in my apron, just as had many during my performance. I gave her a half-moon smile, slid it to him, back to her, said, 'Thank you.'

She put out her hand and I shook it. 'Go well. Follow through.'

My curly student came forward as I turned to leave, and I realised she had watched and witnessed the whole thing. She gave me a sort of bashful smile, all kind of freaked. 'This way,' she told me, indicating with her hand I go before her.

At the threshold of the door, I paused, turned and she just about crashed into me. 'Wait,' I muttered, all stepping around her. I felt the power of my voice when I said to the centre-piece at the table, 'And for serious, no one would give their right arm. Not for anything.'

He for sure looked startled. And he did kind of chuckle.

'I nearly told him where to shove it,' I told my flatmate thickly, face wadded so hard into her linen work smock, my damp skin just about stuck to its weave as I levered myself out of her bosom.

'It sounds like you did already. And good job, too.'

'But I didn't, see? I just really want to go there, see. I don't know, I want to go there more than ever now.'

'Well, you will. If not this year, then next.'

'No.' I shook my head. 'No, I won't go back if they don't take me this year. It's this year—or not at all. I exactly told them *that*.'

She chuckled all sweet, cupped my face as she smoothed the pad of her thumb over my cheek, all kind of like a rubber. 'You have the imprint of linen on your little darlface, sweetie…'

'Imprinting! *That's* it—*that's* what he wants to do to me. Just like we do with the newborn foals, when we stroke them all over, except at their flanks where the jockeys guide them with their heels, see. I nearly said that too—that he wanted to tame my spirit.'

'Well, you're untameable. I should think he saw *that*. Fuck it— maybe you don't want to go there, hey?'

'Hmm,' I said, vaguely, my mind meandering away to other pastures.

'Tell you what—why don't you go for a little snooze?—we were up at sunrise—I had one myself, whilst you were out—and I'll make us some dinner?'

I focused my gaze back at her. 'I'm going to go and find his flat.'

'His flat?'

'The squat.'

'Oh, *his* flat.'

'Yup. I can't just leave it. I need to know.'

'But you don't have the address—I thought?'

'No. But I think I know enough to find it.'

'Well, I'm coming with you then.'

'No, Jessie. I have to do this by myself.'

'I'm not so sure—'

'—well, I am. You're not responsible for me just because you're older, see. I've done a lot of things on my own.' I began toward my room, turned, hands spread. 'But listen—thank you. I appreciate you, huh?'

She made a kind of half-hearted nod, eyes skittish. 'I could wait for you outside. I mean, you could be knocking on anyone's door, right?'

'I know the flat number. Because it was the 23rd when we got together—and he liked the synchronicity. And I liked him saying that—

because we like synchronicity, huh? I'm pretty sure I know the road—see, the area is London Bridge—I've looked it up already in the *A-Z* and it makes sense. I just don't know what the building number is, or what it's called or whatever. But I know it's a council estate, see? Red brick, he said. With those built-in balconies. And he told me some funny story about how his flatmate hung a Mickey Mouse duvet cover in the front room window instead of a curtain—has some sort of sunlight phobia, so it's always closed. He told me enough.'

I scampered into my bedroom, tore off my costume, slipped into my scalloped-edged suede skirt and a men's white vest I had gotten from that Lawrence Corner army salvage place near Warren Street tube. I checked my face in the mirror, wiping beneath my eyes with my knuckles, my attention drawn to the reflection of my friend's collage behind me, which I had owned since her first exhibition at the squat.

I turned, sloped to where it hung on my wall. Looked straight up to the left, located the tiny image cut from a photograph, of a boy's lovely and familiar face—a kid from her youth, way before I had known her. This cut-out photo was the small remnant of Jessie's short-lived and long-treasured romance with him when she was something like fifteen. His head was encircled in golden thread, which looped off to link to a pink dried-up rose petal. Which was me: the rose petal was me, see—I saw this with sudden and searing clarity.

After gazing up at the boy for a maybe a full minute there came a warm sting to my cloudy skies. I blinked hard, pulled myself straight, elevated my length from my crown up. I cleared my throat. 'Now wish me luck,' I said to him, all matter-of-fact. 'With my new crazy mission to forget.'

Pussy Willow

The door was painted a raggedy matt-red, streaky brush marks every-which-way, its small opaque window all reinforced with that metal mesh stuff, emitting not a jot of light from inside. There was no door number but for sure I knew it was the one. To confirm my feeling, the door opposite had a twenty-two on it, the ones on the next floor up, a twenty-four and twenty-five.

I stood outside for quite a while, my feet shifting and scraping on the gritty concrete floor now and again, every sound running up and down the funnel of the staircase all echoey and loud, despite the music and voices I picked up from within the flat. I listened carefully, trying to discern his tone, decided it wasn't there. I crossed to gaze through the narrow low-lying hallway window, watched the trees swaying, waving their high eye-level leaves all kind of joyous at me.

Rapping on the door with tentative knuckles, I was startled when it began to open whilst I was in the act, and I stepped backwards as it pulled away from me, found myself face to face with a girl in maybe her early twenties. She showed a momentary scare, quickly caught a hold of herself, managed some sort of a smile.

'Can I help you?'

I took in her tall bony frame, broad shoulders, her Fifties-looking dress, the red beret atop her ashen bob. Bright red lips. I couldn't seem to find any words, there was something about the way she looked at me, watery-blue eyes all kind of suspicious, seeming to recognise me and not want me there. She had a handbag slung on one shoulder.

'Do you live here?' I said.

There was a stoniness beneath the smile. 'I don't—I'm visiting. Who are you looking for?'

A shadow was moving in the darkened hallway behind her and a lanky kind of a guy loomed over her shoulder, all warmth and welcome, his goatee rushing me with thoughts of Mr Tumnus. His teeth were big, crammed tightly together, and I clocked his fat sideburns. 'You!' he said.

I returned his laugh, which was all inside his nose and chest. 'Me?'

'It's alright, I got this,' he told the woman, giving his head a clippy kind of sideways nod, like he was directing her to leave. He pushed forward, revealing his floral short-sleeved shirt, all fluttery, took a hold of my hand, drew me just about through her, so she had to jump aside, and it really felt I was yanked through the wardrobe and into Narnia. I half-expected his lower body to be that of a fawn, laughed some more when I saw his skinny-fitting thick brown corduroys.

'See ya, Heaven,' he said.

'Oh. Okay. Well, see you then, Wildy. I've got to get going.' Her eyes skimmed to me but she didn't say goodbye—and I don't know why, I felt kind of sorry for her—but couldn't hardly stand her at the same time.

He shut the door, led me into the famous murky living room, its Mickey Mouse drape made ghostly with the sun trying to get in from behind it, Mickey's silhouette all shining through the grotty interior of the duvet cover. 'Look who it is,' Mr Tumnus murmured, breathy-as, to the other couple of blokes there—both of whom rose, all sort of sloppy and slow-motion, lumbering toward me with slidey kind of grins on them. The strong smell of sensi and their glazed bloodshot eyes told me they must be stoned out of their belfries. They introduced themselves— Woodsy, the lazy-eyed film star-looking one—and Hawk, short and round, fluffy-haired, oozing affection, all like a teddy bear.

Hawk kissed my cheek, had a hold of my hand, all nodding. 'We watched you, like, a million times, hanging out in the edit. Loving the vid. Loving it. You are most excellent, most excellent. Stunning.'

'Ah...thanks. Is that where he is? Editing?'

'He's going to be stoked,' Wildy Tumnus was saying, as he sank into a massive beanbag, appeared to be dropping off in an instant with his tightly-packed grin intact.

'He's going to freak,' came Woodsy. He pulled hard on a joint he had between his long fingers, fire-red flaring up and chasing toward his lips.

'He'll freak?' I said.

'He needs to freak,' he bleated through his held-in breath.

'Yeah, c'mon.' The teddy drove dense pincers around my upper arm, began to propel me, all like he was arresting me. 'Let's freak him out.'

'Wait. But where is he? Where are we going?'

'This way…'

He turned me down the corridor, away from the front door. 'He's here?'

I heard muted laughter behind me, felt the hot high breath of it. I felt like I was in an alternate universe, wondered, was I out of it myself, off of all the fumes?

'Shh,' said Teddy. 'C'mon. You gotta keep it down, mate. Or what kind of surprise is the Colonel going to get?'

'The Colonel?'

He bulge-eyed me, all upwards from below me, his face sheened with sweaty excitement. We were at a door and he was levering down the handle, pushing us through it, and of course I got to know as I stumbled into the sudden searing brightness, Hawk yelling, 'Look what the wildcat brought in,' that he was here. Teddy and Woodsy were all cracking up, falling about all over the place, then slumping onto the bed on the floor—which yes, he was in—clutching at themselves and each other, then yelling, 'Bundle!' as they threw themselves on top of him. I stood there, all kind of laughing, kind of relieved, kind of maybe angry. It was a small room, just the bed, a built-in wardrobe, an open suitcase spewing clothes, and little else. A stack of books was by the mattress, and it fell now, knocked in the fray, his copy of *A Clockwork Orange* showing me its illustrated cover: bowler-hatted head on orange ground, just the one eye, its perfect circle all like one of Jessie's washers, eyelashes as spokes on a wheel. I wondered about my dried-up dandelion. He was yelling at them to get off and finally the both of them rolled out of their bundle, flopped with arms splayed, either side of him, all panting, puffy residues of laughter running through them.

He raised himself on his elbows, glorious torso coming out of his scarlet sheets, hips and lengthy legs a mountain range beneath the ancient-looking patchwork quilt. He cracked his chewing-gum grin, all boyish—all the opposite of my truest eternal love—but the flash of that stain, it tugged on my little pink bud. 'Hello you.'

'Hello.'

He ran his bald fingers through his hair, making it stick up the way he liked. 'Aren't you a clever girl?'

I shrugged. I wanted to tell him I didn't care for his vocab. Or his tone.

'Hey fellas,' he said, kicking first one and then the other. 'Get the hell out of here, will ya?'

'Ah man,' came Hawk, straining as he sat up, turning to eyeball him. 'Did that freak you out—did that freak him out—or what?'

Woodsy was staggering to his feet, taking on a fresh slew of laughter.

'Go on, get out.'

They began his bidding, stuck on repeat about freaking him out as they careened to their exit, telling me wow and rad, all friendly. Teddy-bear Hawk paused in the doorway, pointed his finger right at me, literally sang out, all holding an invisible mic, 'Do you wan-na te-e-e-ea?' his voice coming easy-as and lyrical, incongruent with his looks. 'With milk and su-u-gar? C'mon ba-by, how d'you like it?'

Woodsy took to playing air guitar behind him, so I couldn't help the smile snaking itself onto my face. I shook my head, lips sealed, compressing the smile away. My heart was sort of descending.

He swore at them, not so lyrical, directed them to shut the door, and it closed with a snap, their footsteps receding off down the corridor, disappearing into their muffled music.

I stood gazing at him, giving him stones the way that Heaven-person had me. His mossy eyes gazed back, sober-looking, and he held one side of his slender lower lip beneath his front teeth. I felt like I didn't really want to be here now, like I'd seen enough, and I thought about walking right out, I really did. But I didn't. I just stood.

'Hey,' he said. He patted the bed. 'Come here.'

I raised my chin, so I looked down on him even more.

'Schmoobie…' He made a lame-arsed sparky smile, then let it fall away as he sighed out loud, eyes going into his quilt. 'Okay. I get it. This looks bad, eh?'

'Mmm.'

He eyeballed me. 'I got sick.' He indicated where he was as proof, with both hands, palms up.

'O*kay*.'

'I caught something pretty bad in Cuba. I could hardly move. I felt like shit, unbelievable. I thought I was going to die, that bad. They've got me on hefty antibiotics. Look, it's the tail-end now—I'm nearly better.'

'I'm sorry for you. I'm glad you're better.'

'I know, I know, I should have let you know. But you know—'

'—I *know*—'

'—no phone.'

'Hmm…'

He wilted under my gaze. 'Yeah, okay, I could've asked one of the fellas—I know, I've been shit—but at first I was too ill to think straight—and then—then, I don't know, I just felt it was too late—I'd let you down, you were going to be pissed off—it was a mess—*I* was a mess—I *am* a mess.'

I wanted to ask him his age, all sarcastic.

'Look,' he said. 'I know it looks bad but…' He shifted the covers aside, swivelled his legs, feet into the floor. He was wearing pink boxer shorts with big white spots on them. I liked the way his thighs sprouted course kind of sparse hairs. He raised himself to standing. I could tell he was sort of wobbly and that damn smile of mine had another go of insinuating itself onto my lips. I realised I was enjoying myself.

His eyes went moss-soft, a bit dewy, as he stepped to me, stroked one hand all the way from my shoulder down one arm, to take a hold of my compliant fingers. 'Hey, I'm sorry. You know I'm crazy about you. I'm a fool. You're right: there's no excuse but—I mean I was *really* sick—but please...forgive me? Can you? Give me another chance? Schmoobit?'

Again, his hands out—but this time an invitation into his hug. Everything hard in me kind of broke, and I felt myself nodding, spilling my own softness as he took me in his arms with satisfying force, my own arms going about him, fingertips feeling the pleasure of his naked skin. He stooped, kissed my throat. The heat in me rose, my petals opening, the tingles spreading up and through me, and I moved my face, seeking to kiss him, to let go all the tension built up over these weeks. I curled my hand around the back of his head, messaging my desire with directed pressure. He skimmed my cheek with his lips, straightened himself, and we were pushing ourselves into one another. I gave him a shove, made him stumble backwards, so we fell onto his mattress, breathy laughter infused into our yearning.

'Bundle. Bundle,' I said. My hands were all over him. I tore off my vest, sat astride him. His fingers came curled to grab my breasts, then stopped mid-air, tensed into beguiling clawless paws.

'We've got to stop,' he said.

'It's okay—I don't care if they hear us.' I grasped his rude fingers, pushed them into my small mounds of flesh.

'Oh god...schmoobie, please, listen we *got* to stop. I'm serious.

We really *got* to.'

The tenor of his voice, the fear in his face, halted me, hit me all the way into my writhing insides. Everything was snapping shut and shrinking. A mesh of nerves wrapped around my heart. 'What? What is it?'

'I don't want to risk you catching this.'

I slung myself off of him, head all shaking. 'But you're—you're better, you said.'

'But I might still be contagious. *Getting* better I said. That's why I didn't kiss you.'

'Well, why didn't you say before then? Why let us get this far?'

'I didn't mean to. It's just that you—'

'—you can't be blaming me.'

He put his hand on my thigh. I tried not to flinch. 'I know. I'm not. I'm really not. It's my fault. I should have said so immediately. This is a very nasty thing—I would hate you to get it. Aw fuck, I just couldn't resist you.'

I heaved quite a breath. 'Well, what is it then, this thing?'

'Some horrible infection.'

'What kind of infection?'

'Um, well, I don't remember the name. It's...it's in my lungs.'

'And you might have given it to me?'

'Well, no—I'm sure you'll be fine—but, um, you see, this is why I didn't think I should see you—I didn't want to risk...'

'But you didn't tell me that.'

'I know. I didn't think. Look, the course of antibiotics ends in five days—and they'll check me and then we'll know for sure I'm free of the little bastard—I mean, not contagious—ya get me? Schmoobie? And then we can...'

I nodded. I wanted to tell him he was a bit of a prat. I reached all kind of slow, took my vest from where it lay on the floor, slipped it back on. 'I think I better go.'

'Okay.'

'That's it? Okay?'

'I mean, just for now. Or why not stay for a bit—um, have tea—I'll call Hawk, he can—'

'—na-ah.' I said, all wrinkly-nosed.

'Well, just come sit here next to me for a bit, can't—'

'—nah.' All one sharp syllable. If he pat the bed one more time I was about ready to deck him, I didn't care how ill he was.

'Tell me what you've been up to—'

'—it's probably best I just push off, huh. Leave you to rest and that. You do look tired. I think there's some kind of a rash on your belly, huh?'

He flinched, flicked his fingers across his stomach, 'Just a bit,' drew the red sheet over himself, almost up to his chin. 'It was much worse. It's just the end.'

'You think the rash is contagious?'

'No. No, it's not—they told me—the rash is from the antibiotics—don't worry. It's just the kissing really.'

'Well, we could have done it without kissing if you'd told me and I knew…'

I slid myself down the bed, letting my boots bite into his threadbare patchwork, let a square or two tear under my heel. I saw there was a lairy glass vase by the window, all swirly marbled colours, bearing beautiful dried branches of pussy willow, slender and long, like him, like me, like we both together somehow, the furry grey-green flower buds all tender-as, so I felt them right into the heart of me, little explosions of newness and spring. I rose, tucked in my vest, tugged at my skirt to straighten it.

'I'll call you,' he said. 'I will. I'm allowed up tomorrow. Maybe I can come and see you, like the day after? Once I'm a bit stronger.'

'Yeah...maybe.'

'Hey, don't be mad at me. Tell me you're alright.'

I shrugged, smiled. 'Course I'm alright. Why wouldn't I be?'

A Bunch of Violets

I sifted through my rail, pushing back the hangers one after the other, to check out the outfits I was going to wear. There were a lot of changes. This was a mixed designer show for a massive new indoor market-type outlet, a fancy version of the celebrated Kensington Market, which was all worn out now, and scruffy, had been going since sometime in the Sixties. I loved Kensington Market, such a hive of diversity, old and new, antique and tourista; I had been introduced to it when I first came to London, by a kind of boyfriend who had set up a trendy hairdressers there, right when I knew him. This new place was a bit too super-cool, all bright and white, exclusive to hip designers.

We were backstage, set-up in a giant white tent pitched in Kensington Gardens, rows of rails straining with clothes and accessories, endless shoes beneath, all the looks ready and waiting for our rehearsal. The show was a gala opening for the paying public, plus had a massive guest list of fashion editors, journalists, actors, singers, all kinds of celebrities. It was totally sold out. Someone said Twiggy was going to there. I wondered how ol' Twiggy was these days—and if she still looked amazing.

Models were draped all over the place, some made-up already, as was I, others just hanging about, chatting or snoozing, awaiting their turn to be called. Everyone else was full-on busy: makeup and hair crafting their looks, directing their models to gaze at themselves in bulb-framed mirrors above tables heaving with neatly laid kit; dressers, always women, collating the outfits they were assigned to; designers all kind of milling around, excited, agitated, anxious; and the show coordinating team were into directing this and that, testing the music system, the lighting, generally staving off freak-outs, whilst also in solemn conference with the choreographer—our extravagant black dancer-friend from our wild club nights. He was proud to be gay, camp-as, called everything brilliant "fierce".

'Is this for real?' I said to my dresser, unhooking a black floor-length tubular stretch dress from the rail. 'Tell me there's something to go underneath?' I slipped my fingers inside the neck, wiggled them at her through the perfectly finished cut-out breast holes.

'Oh,' she said, looking a bit startled. 'I don't know. Goodness. I don't suppose there is...unless there's something here.' She was an older woman, short, stocky, with tied-back sandy hair and metal-framed glasses, the type you got in a two-for-one deal it looked like. We sort of knew each other, she had dressed me quite a few times, and she looked kind of worried for me as she started checking through the rail for sign of a missing piece.

A sigh came over me. I gave her a wry look. 'So I'm supposed to go out there with my boobs all just sticking out? All nudey nipples and everything?'

She took the dress from me, opened it up at its polo neck, peered inside. 'Golly, it would seem so…nothing here…'

'Well, I'm not wearing it. They can't make me. Can they? I never agreed to this.'

'I don't know.'

'They can't. I'll just refuse to do the show at all if they try to— they can get someone else. I'm going to call my agent. It's abuse if they make me. Don't you think? It's abuse, huh?'

She held me in kind brown eyes, all behind her specs. 'I'm sure we can sort it out. Why don't we ask if you might swap with a girl who doesn't mind?'

'You think someone will be happy to wear it?'

'Yeah. Girls go topless, don't they? On the beach?'

'I go topless—on the *beach*. I even have in films and that. But it's totally different—boobs is all you'll see in the sea of this black mantle. Look, even the arms are full-length. It'll be just face and boobs. I just don't want to—'

'—okay, come on. Let's go talk to one of the crew, shall we? It's fair enough if you're not comfortable with your boobs sticking out on the catwalk, eh?' She giggled suddenly. 'It is pretty funny, though— in a way.'

'Hmm. Sexist.'

'But the designer is a woman. Perhaps it's celebrating the beauty of the breast? Freedom or something. *Burn the bra* woman's liberation taken to new heights?' She elbowed me. 'I'm surprised, knowing you, you don't want to wear it. Considering. It's rebellious, a statement against society.'

'I get what you're saying—I *like* what you're saying—but sorry, no, it's not for me—this statement or whatever. Not today. I bet it will be in all the papers tomorrow though, huh? I'll bet you anything.'

We went and found the boss coordinator, who I worked with a lot, and he was easy-as about it, told us to go ahead with the swap as my dresser suggested. Something from the same designer, he said.

There came two rehearsals, eating lunch in between—then makeup and hair were touching us up and the audience out front were a buzz of chatter, all intermingled with the pre-show music. We stood in a line backstage in our first outfits, the front of house lights fading to black, spotlights coming up and splashing brightly on the first girl as she glided above the throng, each of us held back at the threshold of the catwalk by a coordinator either side, in their head-sets, until the moment they were cued to send us out. Different designers had different music, the clothes demanding their own attitude, an expression of character—it was how it was then, not like now, when pretty much every walk is blank— sometimes we had to dance as we walked, others, to be cool, demure, sexy, whatever the outfit gave unto. The girl wearing my boob-dress played it kind of spicy when I thought it would have been better all puritanical, for contrast, but it was her bag, and I was relieved not to be wearing it.

The show was flamboyance, play, politics, joie de vivre. We posed and twirled at the end of the catwalk for the mob of photo-journalists, lights popping and flashing, the cameras devouring and ratifying—oh, mirroring back!—our fabulous fashionable glamour. *Dahling*.

Turning off of the catwalk all casual, I scampered fast down the set-up steps, reaching arms from invisible bodies assisting my safe passage. I ran to my rail, all pulling off my earrings, was met by my dresser, raising my arms as she yanked off my top. She bent, undid the fine golden buckles of my heels. I unzipped my skirt, let it fall, stepped out of the shoes and skirt at once. I stood in just my g-string, briefly conscious of the three lecherous male models who always and openly watched us girls as if we were their divine right. I knew they played some sort of game, picked up different girls all the time, those innocent of their appetites, in clubs too, then dumped them after sleeping with them, just gratifying their greedy egos. They were idiots, that was for sure. My dresser threw my discarded skirt and silk sweater over the rail, in the same instance grabbing the crop top she had ready for my next outfit, helping me into it. As I adjusted it, she had me step into my new skirt, a kind of flamenco-looking one, all flared and frilled, did up my zip, passed me fresh earrings, from behind me put on a necklace of plastic fruits, then helped me into the red wedges for the outfit. I checked myself in the nearest full-length mirror, tugged and adjusted, took on the necessary attitude.

As I waited in line I was perfected and preened by designer, makeup, hair. I was on again, off again—and so. Until the finale came and we all of us streamed down the catwalk in a celebratory rush, the front-row V.I.P.s below us clapping, all smiling wide, whooping and whistling even, the public behind them in a kind of rhapsody, photographers all hustling for their shots, so you got to feel on fire. And then you guzzled champagne backstage as if it were water.

We unwrapped me out of my outfit, an irreverent take on a wedding dress, just paint-spattered tulle all wound around me, tight as can be, my dresser getting me to pirouette as she folded up the long length of fabric with another dresser assisting her. We laughed and chattered, took our time, then kissed each other's cheeks in goodbye, myself then kissing just about everyone, before I went whizzing off to town in all my heavy makeup, my hair all big and back-combed, Sixties glamorous.

I got off the tube through the crush of rush hour people, rose up from the depths on the escalators of the Piccadilly line, straight away found a payphone in the ticket hall, dropped my ten pence piece into the void. I told him I was here already; it had been brilliant, a roaring success, he should have been there—but his loss.

'I know,' he said. I could hear him tugging on a joint, breath all held, voice constrained, as he continued, 'You know, I tried—but it was impossible to get away with this deadline. I'm gutted. So how long are you going to be?'

'Maybe twenty minutes or so. I'm going to pick up something to eat on the way. You want anything?'

I bounded up the station stairs onto the street, crossed Charing Cross Road, traversed Leicester Square, hit Wardour Street, and on an impulse, decided, bugger the food, I wasn't really hungry yet, I felt high-as and wanted to see him. I was ringing on his buzzer within minutes.

It was answered immediately. 'Hello?' The voice of the receptionist.

'Hello Julia. It's me.'

'Hello sweetie. Come on up. I'm literally leaving so I won't be seeing you—but maybe catch you coming out of the lift?' She buzzed me in, saying, 'Want me to let him know you're here?'

'Nah,' I said. 'Don't worry. He knows I'm coming.'

He was on the fourth floor, but I chose not to bother with the lift, just went haring on up the stairs, two at a time, pretending to myself I was some kind of action hero, my energy fuelled by all the fun—of now—and of kind of "just now"—of this very game and the fashion show and the audience. The lift passed me, heading upwards. I came into this lovely sort of feeling, turning up one flight into another, of all expanding out of my body, of being bigger than me, of my atoms joining with the air; I was attuned to the daisy chain, linking into the many times I had realised this, myself as a part of all that is; the absolute essence of being—all pure consciousness—just coming forth, riding through me—simply because it could. I'm a part of the stairs, I thought, and the building and the blue sky beyond, yes, the stars and the planets, I am matter made up of infinitesimal units of energy that has cycled forever. I am eternal; my uncle was right. I felt a flush of pure love for him and all he had taught me, felt a bloom of love for his Buddha too, before I could feel any hate, and even for science, which was demonstrating we hardly had a clue about atoms and molecules and that an observer could influence an outcome on electrons, and all stuff about the unified quantum field I could hardly understand intellectually, but just *knew* when I tuned in like this. Our power of influence had to be greater than we realised; we must be connected energetically to everything—or how else? As I reached my destination, the lift door slammed shut and I caught a glimpse of Julia through the skinny oblong window, shared a smiley wave, watched her begin her descent.

I was just raising my fist to the door, hand already on the handle, when I felt it turn, began laughing, thrusting myself inward, all expecting his face to meet me in the opening. I fell right into a woman, sprang back to find myself smeared by déjà vu—only it wasn't déjà vu, because it really was a repeat, almost exact.

I stared at her, all kind of tight. 'Hi.'

'Hello.' Her red lips looked unnatural in the smile she produced. 'I'm just on my way out.' She moved forward so I had to scurry back some more. 'See ya.' And *she* wasn't waiting for the lift either.

I tore through the empty reception, pushed open the door to the edit suite, enclosed myself into the blurry slur of the super-sloweddown music in the room. The air was heavy with marijuana. His back was to me, his focus on the two large screens in front of him, digits around the sizable knob with which he could perfect each cut to a frame, his spliff protruding from between his first two fingers. I saw there was a little bunch of violets on his desk, all in a pretty white wrapping. He turned as the door clicked shut from the weight of my body up against it, his face going all surprised and—what?—a flash of some kind of—fear?—guilt maybe—this quickly appropriated by his aped chewing-gum grin.

'Schmoobie.'

'Yeah. Schmoobie…'

'You got here fast.' He took a pull on his joint, laid it into the little groove in his ashtray.

'I thought we could order a pizza, see.'

He was getting up from his swivel chair, moving toward me, arms out. 'You look gorgeous. Amazing. Wow, I really missed something, eh?'

'You really did. But I didn't.'

He went to take me in his embrace, stooping to kiss my throat on the way, scudding his lips across my cheek. 'One more day—we get the test results, and I can kiss you for real.'

'Hmm…'

'You're driving me crazy.' He pushed his length up against mine, all squashing me into the door, breathy-as. 'Can't you tell, schmoobit?'

'*I* didn't miss anything though, see.'

'What?'

'I saw her—your friend...'

'Oh.' His body went still.

'Bumped right into her. You didn't get her out of here fast enough, see.'

Voice all into the veneered panel door, he said, 'Shit. You saw her.'

'Hmm.' I gave him a bit of a shove with my hips and he had to step back to keep his balance. I eyed him with the stones she had

61

trained me to use. 'Who is called *Heaven* anyway? I bumped into her at the flat too, by the way, when I came the other day. Visiting, she told me. I guess it was you, huh? The visiting. Which I knew, of course, already, all along. I'm not an idiot.'

'Okay.' He rubbed his face, sighed, rude fingertips teasing me. 'Okay—I was hoping not to get into this—but I'm going to have to explain.'

'I'll say.'

'She's my *ex*-girlfriend. From years ago.'

'Who is still totally into you.'

'Yeah…'

'And what? It looks like you're into her—'

'—no—'

'—I think you are.'

'No—it's just she—'

'—you want it all, huh? Me and her.'

'No, I-I just can't control her—I mean, she needs me and—'

'—she *needs* you? Well, you're encouraging her. How is that okay? Any of it?'

He stood, all like a little boy being told off by a teacher, kind of forlorn. His lips were tight-as, I could see he was biting on them from the inside. He pushed a knuckle into his cheek, took to chewing on that too.

'You *are* still into her. Are you doing stuff with her?'

'No. God, no.' He sighed. 'I just feel sorry for her. She does need me, I mean it. Seeing me makes her feel better.'

'Are you aware how pathetic that sounds? What kind of ego are you?'

'Ah come on, schmoobit. Don't give me a hard time. I'm trying to do my bit. Trying to do good. Help someone I used to be with, who I care about—in a totally unbiblical fashion. I was her first boyfriend and other guys have given her a hard time and she…' He made a kind of shrug.

'Unbiblical?'

'I don't fancy her a bit.'

'Well, like I said, you're encouraging her then—*if* nothing else is *really* going on—how can you not be? You must know that. It would be kinder to draw a line.'

'I've tried… You know, she hurts herself if I don't—she cuts—but listen, she knows about you. She knows you're my girlfriend. She knows I'm completely potty for you. She accepts that—she and I— we're just friends.'

I nodded, a sigh coming from way down under, all the way from Australia it felt like. 'I don't think she accepts me, actually. She clearly can't stand me. Can't stand you've got a girlfriend, for sure. And you know what? It sounds to me like she's—what do you call it?— yes, emotionally blackmailing you, no? With all this cutting herself rubbish.'

'Yeah, well, it's difficult for her.' He reached for my hand and I let him take it, all kind of stiff, in his. 'It's not rubbish—it-it's bad, scares me for shit. She's been to hospital for it. And one has to be compassionate, caring—supportive, don't you think? Look, I don't see her much, honest. She's been around more these last couple of weeks because she turned up at the flat when I was really sick, and, you know, well, she looked after me. She came and brought me food and made soup and crap. That's all. Usually, I really only see her maybe every couple of months or so. I told her today she has to cool it. I'm better now—and you're back. She won't be coming around. It was a shame you saw her just now.'

'I don't know about that. It's better that I did. Otherwise I would think you're up to something. You've got to be honest. Otherwise what's the point?'

'Yes, you're right. But I didn't mean—I mean, I didn't lie.'

'I think maybe you like her being into you, huh?'

He raised his eyebrows, head turning as his wide mossies rolled, a hefty sigh coming through vibrating raspberry lips. 'That's a bit harsh.'

I shrugged. 'It's a kind of harsh situation. For me. I'm not so sure I'm comfortable with it.'

Some kind of sparkle came into his eye. 'Schmoobie feeling jealous?' He made pouty lips, all kind of girlie. 'Come here, you.' And he reached for me so I had no choice, wrapped his arms around my waist like a corset, tugging me into him hard. My body just started up on its own, all responsive, tugging and yelping deep inside, but I did my best to hide it. 'Nothing to be jealous of, my schmoobit. Nothing, ya hear? She's nothing to me. I am totally into you. You've transformed me—I told you that already. I'm a different man. I want you and only you. You've got to believe me.'

A Venus Flytrap

I was twirling all over the woodblock flooring, skidding around in my big boots—just me with Woodsy's girlfriend—while a student-y crowd stood about the spacious collage hall, bopping their heads, kind of standstill-grooving to Wildy's drums, Woodsy's crashing guitar, Jon's base, and Hawk's easy high-pitched voice, all rocketing through the sound system. As the song tailed into its end, I ran to the front, skipping and jumping, screaming like a proper fan, larking arms reaching toward Hawk, his laughing response all sliding about his sweat-sheened teddy-bear face.

My assistant director blurred towards me, nudged into my side, thrust his full-size bottle of bourbon into my hand. His sparsely haired wrist protruded rudely from his too-small Harrington cuff. I took a big slug. All holding my eye, he poked his finger into the rip in the thigh of my red lacy tights, on purpose shooting glittersparks, vivid pink and purple, right into my hungry bud.

He leaned into me, 'Are you up yet? Do you feel it?'

'I'm always up.'

He laughed, well delighted. 'My little kook. And…?'

'I don't know. I feel great. But I don't know if it's your pill. What about you?'

'Yeah,' he said. And he made a kind of cross-eyed lazy version of his chewing-gum smile, conveying to me the ecstasy this stuff was named for. He had gotten the E, he called it, in New York, on their stop-over from Cuba, a few pills secreted in his sock, he'd said. His fleshy fingertip was still stuck in my hole, all stroking my skin under the flowery lace, like he couldn't get enough. He for sure looked out of his tree, his smile radiating all rapturous. 'Maybe a half takes longer—maybe you should have taken the whole one.' Something pinged in his mind, flashed into his black-holed mossies. 'Come on, I know how to bring you up.'

I scampered after him, keen-as, and we slipped into the ladies' together, snuck into a cubicle, where he extracted a tiny paper wrap from his wallet, took out a credit card and a ten pound note. His bald fingers untucked and opened the fold with loving care. Using the corner of the card as a miniature shovel, he laid a chunk of white powder onto the toilet cistern, chopped through it with the card edge, divided it and made two hefty white lines, myself all rolling the note into a tube.

'Go on,' he told me, indicating with his chin. 'You go first.'

I bent over the lines, stuck the money straw up one nostril, closed off the other, and sucked mine up in a hard snort. I came up smiling, handed him the straw. 'Wow.' I sniffed intensely a few times. My nostril burned inside, all satisfying. I took a big swig of the bourbon, felt its hot fumes at my throat as he pulled his line into his body. He took a glug from the bottle, smoothed his indecent-looking fingertip—which sent further glitter-bombs into my little cunt—smoothed it across the area where the blow had disappeared, me joining him uninvited, the two of us running the dust under our upper lips, along the gumline, all grinning at each other. I already felt my temples expanding, a tingling through my scalp—and my upper lip was going numb. 'It's good stuff, huh?' I said.

He made an indication with wide eyes, finger flicking the tip of his own nose, but before I could fully comprehend, he made a swoop at me, tongue running across my nostril, hot and wet. 'Got it,' he said.

I felt myself laid wide open, a sensual surge uprising from the floor. He whispered all into my ear, breath heated and moist, and I felt I was in some sort of fantastical dispersion; he whispered he wanted me, was mad for me, I was making him crazy, he couldn't stand it, I was gorgeous, I was a dream, hands all groping for my boobs. His spit morphed into a charged ring at my nostril. And we were kissing before I knew it, hungry-as, all hard and soft—a dirty bitterness from the coke—my inner body writhing, swelling, arching—

'—hey.' I pulled back, neck a mass of prickles, the flat of my fingers pressing into my lips—*oh! fingertips! lips!* all bloating into each other, intense, like this was brand new and—*my god, stunning!* Even as my heart was thumping flags in my ears. 'But they told you we can't do it yet—we shouldn't be doing this yet.' My voice sounded all voluptuous and far away inside of me.

'We *can* kiss.' He held my upper arms in a kind of vice, voice a mumbled blur. He exhaled, all sticky-sweet-sour, into my face. 'It's not contagious when we kiss now. We just can't have sex.'

'Are you sure? Are you sure it's okay to kiss? I mean, how can that change?' Every word I said sent renewed ripples of delight through every nerve-ending.

'It's fine, schmoobie, we're good. Definitely.'

'But didn't your rash get worse again and everything? You sure?' I was smiling all the way into myself.

His eyes went filmy, red crept up his cheeks. 'Yeh, of course I'm sure. What do you take me for?' His voice was liquorice-soft. 'I'm not going to risk it, schmoobie.' He produced his grin, the stain seeming to lick me right between my legs, wrap itself round my heart, steal from my lungs. His mossies were heavy-lidded, pupils gaping. 'You look amazing,' he murmured.

'But how long—' I fell back against the cubicle wall. My insides ached, a sort of thrumming calling, '—*really* how *long* is this going to go on for? It's been weeks now…'

'Just another three days, I told you. A two-week course, remember? You know the first course wasn't strong enough, eh? The rash is from these buggers again—they assured me—I told you. These are really mega boom. *Four* days once they check me.'

I nodded, found I couldn't help giggling and feeling all kind of brilliant despite what he was saying. 'Hey but—hey, I'm sure you're not supposed to drink when you take antibiotics. Won't it interfere or something?'

'S'fine. Just makes you more out of it.'

'It better be fine—this is making me mental—and the kissing is making it harder, don't you—*oh!*' I pressed my forefinger into the skin of my throat, drew a line downward into the little pit between my collar bones. 'I feel the toot. I can taste it going down. Oh, it's nice…and, god, I feel…I'm kind of rushing inside, all like liquid candyfloss.' My hands slipped down his sides and I went electric-as, spasmed by those rushes, as if it were he touching me—all over. My beautiful flower swelled so I could feel it; it for sure sprang with dew. 'Oh. Oh my god…'

'It's got you. Fantastic. I got you.'

He smoothed his hands around my face, bent into me, sucked my lips into his, his tongue pushing between them. Our kiss grew, the heat of me spreading into the cubicle, feeling to suffocate me. He left my lips, travelling down my throat, lifted my t-shirt and fell upon my breasts. I felt consumed by the high, my body all releasing, going into layers, advancing my sense of expansion and I felt like I was floating up and out of myself from the chest—*oh yes!* from the heart. And a river was flowing through me. Someone came into the ladies', a couple of girls, talking to each other. They went into the cubicles either side of us, the sound of their wee quite merry. They left. He crouched onto his knees, pushed my skirt up, tugged my tights and knickers down, his tongue finding me, sliding its wetness over me and I pushed my hips into his face, explosions coming soft and rippling, all up and through me, all from the exquisite intensity in that one bright place. Women kept coming in and out, loud splashes of our friends' music echoing about the tiled walls each time the main door opened. I ooo-ed and aaah-ed, all keeping my voice inside, and when he used his finger too, it was all I could do to stay on my feet, just about sinking to the floor, so he lifted my hips, turned me, guiding me onto the loo seat, pushing his splayed hand into my bared breasts, his focus and attention right into me, until waves came and I was clinging to his shoulders, containing the cries I wanted to free.

We left the toilets, every movement causing my body to feel optimal, in stunning cellular awakening—in some kind of absolute now-ness—as we came back onto the dance floor, all holding hands and boogie-ing together in the sprung crowd of dancers. I was totally enough. *Everything* was enough. Life was alive in every eye I caught; love was alive. And somehow I was running, weaving. I realised I was screaming through my laughing and he was chasing me, and I was running into the outside, into the surrounding gardens, galloping over the undulating lawn, slowing, letting him catch a hold of me. His arms came around my waist from behind, tucked me into the long curve of him, and we fell together into the soft turf, the whisky bottle with us. It didn't even hurt when I landed on it. We tumbled and kissed.

He hustled us into some bushes, sent his mouth over—and into—my many writhing undulations in a languorous trance that opened up and went on and on, maybe hours, in which the highest high faded, the rushes disappeared, but all my nerve-endings still felt in resonance with some darling unfolding, a sort of calmer ecstasy all washing me with satisfaction, with ease—and yes, with the endorphins of love.

The music from the gig spent itself and people were leaving, legs and chatter crashing past us. There were distant sounds of clearing up, of equipment packed and loaded into the bands' hire van. We supped on the bourbon whisky, relished its heat, tooted a corner of coke. The hall went dark, a heaven of silence descending. An occasional purr of distant traffic. We, in that Aladdin's cave of bushes. I kissed his naked chest, he let me, but when I neared his belly I felt fine lines of tension within him. My hand scudded over his groin. There was no hardness even though noises came from him all reflecting his pleasure. I slid my fingers into the line of his boxer shorts. And then his hand came and clutched mine, stayed me, insistent.

'No,' he said. 'I really don't think you should—we really mustn't.'

'But just touching you.'

'It's a bad idea.'

'Oh.'

He sat up, bringing me with him. Twigs snapped, stuck into my tights, biting at my skin. He drained the bourbon. 'Don't be offended about...you know...Mr floppy. It's just the drugs.'

'I know. I'm not.'

'You know I'm potty about you.'

'Mmm.'

He fiddled in the pocket of his jacket down beside him, brought out a soft-pack of cigarettes. He lit one. I watched it flare as he tugged on it, full and hard, several times. 'Yeahhh...that brings me back up...' He proffered the fag to my lips, still between his fingers. 'Take a draw. You'll see what I mean.'

I did, and a sweeter rush, of gentler spirit, greeted me. I made a sigh.

'Nice?'

'Yeah.'

He made up a spliff then, chugged, pushed himself up against a small tree trunk, patted his chest. I rested back into him, all dreamy and pleasant. We smoked the spliff and all kinds of lovely sensations ran through my blood.

Light started to grow around us. I gazed through the undergrowth, saw how the dawn was cracking open the sky. Something in me just seemed to split, like seams under strain, a weight coming into my belly, my heart too.

'What really happened?' I said, my voice kind of disembodied, all like someone else's.

'Huh?'

'What happened? Out there, in Cuba?'

'What do you mean?' His voice was like someone else's too.

I slid my bum, swivelled on my hips to face him. 'Something...'

Or maybe this voice was really him and the voice I thought I knew wasn't true. Or I knew all along he had a voice that wasn't true and was only just letting myself believe it. I waited for his reply, watching him. I saw how his dried-up mossies grated about all everywhere down low. He stuck his knuckle into his cheek, drove the flesh between his molars. A bit of a rattle came out of his throat, all like he took a breath to say something but found just dead steam.

'Did something happen—with another girl? Why don't you want me to touch you?'

'You know why.'

'Yeah...' He met my eye briefly, managed a half-arsed smile, the stain some kind of an offense. 'I do,' I said. 'I think I do know why. I feel it. I think you're not telling me something.' My energy began an uncomfortable spiral upward, so my ears went light, the heart of me heavy and pounding in them. He was biting on his pulled-in lips. There came the pathetic sting of tears—I blinked them away. 'You might as well tell me.'

He put his hand, all busting fingertips, onto my forearm. 'Schmoobie...'

'Go on, then.'

'Shit. This stuff is some kind of truth serum, this ecstasy shit...'

'So I'm right?'

'Someone in New York said they developed it for some kind of couples therapy...'

'Couples therapy? This is not—'

'—I know. I just mean—'

'—you just mean you have no choice but to tell me the truth on this stuff. Is that it?'

He kind of nodded. 'I don't know. I mean, *no*—I *want* to tell you, that's it. I just want to come clean and start afresh, you know?' He went to take hold of my hand but I pulled it away. He actually held my eye instead, a surprising openness in his own. 'Listen. I'm really sorry...' He was all shaking his head, all sincere. 'I never meant for it to happen. I didn't plan it. I didn't ask for it. It was them—I had gone up to bed and they sent this girl to my room. They thought it was funny. You know, I was pretty out of it—the cocaine there—it's fucking pure—and I'd been drinking mezcal and—'

'—a girl? What do you mean a girl?'

'You know—a-a girl. They paid her.'

'You mean a—a prostitute?'

'Yup.'

'A prostitute?' The thumping in my ears was massive, pirated my whole body, then was outside of my body too, so the air and the ground and the bushes were gyrating. 'You slept with a prostitute?'

He nodded, eyes falling into the earth.

'But you *had* a choice. So what, they sent her up to your room? You didn't have to do it, did you? You could've just said no. Sent her away. Why didn't you?'

'I don't know.'

'You liked it, huh?' He said nothing and I was intent on getting his eye back. 'You think she wanted you, wanted you to—to fuck her—do you? Huh? Huh?' I kicked out, struck his shin. He looked up, all startled, kind of afraid. 'And what about the lame-arsed declaration you made to me before you went—that I didn't even ask f—'

—this sudden surge of chaos spewed out of me, all kind of crazed yelling, fists flying, my inner thumping externalised into actual blows into his chest, his shoulders—and he had a hold of my wrists, was fighting me—I was uncannily strong, managed to strike him with his own hands atop mine—You lying bastard. You pig. You weak, pathetic—he was yelling over me, trying to soothe me—all, I'm sorry and I'm mad about you and please schmoobie please—until he kind of swept his arms around me, tore me into him, held me against him as I thrashed and blinded, him begging me to Stop it stop it please I'm sorry

I'm sorry I feel terrible I've hated this I didn't know what to do please...

The heat of my rage and hurt and confusion slimed me in a coat of wet, all everywhere, and I was curled against him, wailing, whimpering and he was rocking me, begging me to be okay, to come back to him, he would make it up to me, he was *sorry*.

I couldn't believe I was in his arms, but I couldn't seem to want to get out of them somehow. It was like he was one of those plants, a Venus fly trap, that lures insects with their delicious nectar, then never lets them go, consumes them for sustenance. I nuzzled my nose all into the gap between his girly shirt collars, sniffing him. 'But what?' I murmured. 'Did you make it all up then, about being sick, and the antibiotics and the doctor's and everything?'

'No. Oh shit... I thought you must realise. I caught something from...'

I pushed myself off of him, all eyeballing him. My whole body felt ballooning and somehow it felt beautiful, exquisite even, in all the suffering, sort of expansive to the enth extreme, so the light shone through the dark and my atoms and mind buzzed, all up again. 'What did you catch? What is it?'

'It's NSU.'

'An NSU? What's that?'

'It's a—it isn't bad. It's fully treatable. But sometimes they're not sure of the best antibiotic. And that's why I'm on this second course. I feel shit about it. I feel shit about myself. And about you. It's been killing me. Because I've changed—wanting you has changed me.'

'But what does it mean, NSU? Are you saying it's a venereal disease? That's it, isn't it?'

'Non-specific urethritis.'

'What's that? A sexually-transmitted disease then?'

He nodded, mossies seeding the dry earth. 'In this case, yes. It's an inflammation of my urethra—the tube that carries the pee from the bladder down my prick. I got it from…her.'

'You are…' I said, my head all shaking, heat from inside of me blubbing all glorious down my cheeks. 'You lied to me all this time. And kept me. And maybe compromised me—how can I know? I'm going to have to get myself checked, huh? I hate that—I just hate that.' I jumbled myself to my feet, having to crouch in the hide. 'I'm going. I need to go home.' I crawled, pulling myself through the sticks, stumbled as I got to my feet, reeling all over the place.

He was right behind me, breaking the world. 'I'll see you home. You can't go alone—not like this.'

'Well I can.' A lame attempt at fending him off, falling back onto the grass on my bum, splat out onto my back. I gazed, all haze, into the misty-looking sky. 'You're just not—are y

    i see my reflection in the blue of his eyes in the black of his pupi

ou?'

'I *am*,' he s

    a tiny me made knowabl

aid.

    through hi

'You have no idea,' I said. 'But I knew, I knew yo
    grass soft and prickly

u weren't what you seemed, the moment you went in th
    he hard within m

e-the

    flecks of my bloo

e helicopter.' I realised I had made tiny rivers down my temples, was watering his traitorous seeds and moss would spring here wee

    red against the gree

ks after I was go

        and the tender-blue flowers of the speedwe

ne.

His voice came surprised. 'The helicopter?'

I felt my muscles thrashing about inside, all trying to get up, my limbs not responding. 'I can't move,' I told him.

'Okay, look, I think you better take a little bump.'

'What about the other half?' I wailed. 'I want my other half of ecstasy.' The tears kept streaming.

'I took it already.'

'You took it? When?'

'I dunno. Before we went in the loos.'

'I want the ecstasy.' I managed to raise my head to look at him where he was kneeling now, next to me, but he went spinning off and my skull crashed right back into the earth. 'Oh god...I feel...everything's spinning...oh god...'

He was fiddling. I made out he was taking his stash from his wallet, opening it, all focused. His credit card corner rose to his own nose, and he snorted hard. 'Here,' he said, veering into me. 'Come on. This will sort you out til we get you home.' He lifted my head, directed the little pile of snow beneath my nozzle. 'Sniff. Come on. Big sniff. That's it. Good girl. Hang on—' he dug his card into the open wrap again, thrust it below my other nostril '—okay, again—big sniff. Good. You're going to be alright. Just give this a few minutes...'

Lolling beside me, he rolled another joint. I saw how the strands of tobacco looked alive in the Rizla as he crumbled his hash into it. He sparked it up and we shared it, tugging the smoke into our lungs like zealots. All creeping wispy fingers were floating right the way into my blood, my blood growing capillaries into the air so I could actually see them, neon pink and labyrinthine.

'I hear music,' I murmured. 'Is there an orchestra?'

He got me up, put his arm around my waist, all holding me against him, got me to walk. I stumbled for a while, inhabited by weakness. I think we took another bump. Or two. Maybe three. 'What about H?' I said to him. 'What about horse?'

'Horse?

'Eliot's horse…boys' feet crush it up in Afghanistan…'

'Yeh. I don't have any horse. I don't do heroine.'

'Where is it? Let's have some.'

'I don't do it.'

'Yes, you do. I know you took it the night before we went to Iceland. That's why you were fucked up that morning on the flight, huh? See, I know these things.'

'Fucking Tristan—he told you, right? He's such a jealous fucker. He was making aplay for you, I knew it. He has a girlfriend too.'

'I wouldn't say too much about that, see?'

'He's a tosser.'

'So are you.'

'Look, I don't do heroine—as a rule. This was a one-off. And I only smoked it. It wasn't mine.'

'I smoked it.'

'You did?'

'Once. But not on purpose. And Eliot never let me near it again…'

'Who's Eliot?'

'My friend. You're lucky he's away in America or he would totally beat you up. I'm not kidding. He's massive and he would beat you to smithereens.'

Somehow we were at the road and he told me to stand straight, was hailing a black cab. God knows why, but I was laughing as I climbed in. I let myself drop into the luxurious black seat as he gave the cabbie my address. The sensation of the moving vehicle was nice.

'Never mind,' I said. 'Huh? Never mind me.'

'What's that?' he said.

I shrugged, sank further into the seat. 'Never mind.' He got a hold of me, yanked me into him, all like a ragdoll, his arms around me, jostled me so my back rested against his chest. He was talking to me but all I could make out was his hum, along with the rattle and drone of the taxi. There was sort of a fantastic music, all other-worldly and deathly, and my body was a part of it, heart the rhythm, and I was enveloped in a symphony, full-on. And I was on my bed, crouched over a book, sucking up a fat line. I didn't have any clothes on and he was fully dressed—I seemed to be laughing—or was I cryi—I was shrieking—and *whoa!* my body was all falling away from me, all down below me, throwing itself back into the mattress—I was looking down at myself—this girl down there, jolting and convulsing, her face in a spasm—he was getting hold of her tongue and she was gnashing his fingers to shreds—all convulsing and jolting—I was watching them, from way up high—then I was whizzing off—*yes!* it was an orange-fizzing morning sky—and I was above the building, looking at the roof, going higher, up into black, with the moon, way above the world, gazing at the beauty of it, this blue planet floating in space and—*oh wow! weeeee!* I went flying around the whole circumference of the world, saw the whole shape of Australia, felt myself playing footsies with Robin Remick, felt him nuzzle my neck, my body ecstatic, an unkissed girl, all innocent—then all the black went light, I was in a field of bright—a huge pair of eyes was looking into me, all pale grey as a clouded sky, and I realised the eyes were mine—I was looking at me and hands came, my hands, held themselves up, so I put my hands against my hands, like in a mirror, but felt the warmth of them too: I love you, I said to me. There is great love here for you, *here* for you, here for you, always here for—I was back in the room, floating just below the ceiling—she was jolting and convulsing—and he was darting to the door, yelling yelling yelling. His fingers were bleeding. I could taste it. And Jessie was tearing in, in a baggy t-shirt, shoving him aside, coming to me, bending over me.

'Darling? Darling?' She took a hold of my shoulders, stayed me, my hips bouncing to the music of my blood in my ears. 'This is *not* epilepsy,' she was yelling, all jarring her head toward him. 'What did you give her? You cock. What is it? What did you take?'

'I don't know, I don't know…' was all he seemed to say.

And I was looking up at her, into her golden eyes, everything still. My head totally still. Silent. Utter beauty. She was saying all kinds of soothing words to me. She was waiting, gazing into me. 'Darling? My little darlface? Are you alright?' I felt my lips move, a click of spit. My tongue was loose. My jaw, slack-as, was sliding itself slowly back and forth, my mouth half open, my eyes wide, fixed into hers.

She flicked her sights to him, where he stood in the doorway. 'I think you better go. *Now*.'

Rose Petal Wings

I sat curled over myself, nude-as, on the wooden floor, my face tilted toward her. I watched how her pencil flew all smooth and easy in her practiced hand, making the marks that were the outlines of my body. I could tell she was quite blissy, her sense of freedom expressed in her simple action, the lack of judgment, as she took one blank page after another, letting the last fall in a jumbled pile beside her. She barely looked at the paper as she drew, her sights intense upon the forms I was making. I shifted my position every two or three pieces, now on my knees, now lounging on an elbow; we two in a near-silent tandem, until she sighed, all satisfied, laid down her pencil. 'Time for a break methinks. A stretch and a cup of tea, my darlface?' she said, all through her yawning.

'Some cake,' I said.

I raised myself to standing, arms sailing way up, all linked by my hands, arcing my body to one side.

'Wait,' she said, excitement coming high in her voice. 'Let me...' She took up the thick book next to her, one of those old brown-backed ones she loved to use, where the beautiful wide-spaced font became a meeting point with her image. The words mattered to her; sometimes she would later ring some; and she chose the books carefully, for both content and quality of paper. She eyed me, glided her pencil about the thick matt leaf, this one almost like blotting sheets—she liked the way it sort of gripped the graphite, subtlety slowed the momentum of her sure firm strokes.

I shifted my position as she turned the page, curved over to my other side. I mooched gently across the room, giving her brief walking poses. Reaching the threshold of the door to the kitchen, I flung my arms up, turning to face her as I grabbed the upper part of the doorframe, swung myself through all laughing, marking the glory of our play together.

'Starving,' I said.

'Stay,' she said. 'I love it.' She drew me super-fast as I laughed some more. 'And again. Do it again. Afresh. I love the sense of energy. Of motion.' I dropped my arms, threw them up again, letting my weight drive me toward her, my hands keeping me locked in the doorframe as she described me with free marks, eyes intent on me. 'Oh!' she said. 'What joy!'

I went naked into the kitchen, never mind the window. I put the kettle on and took out the carrot cake she had baked, transferring it onto a plate, unpeeling the greaseproof paper from its flanks. She drew me whilst I went about it all.

'You remember how I used to draw too?' I said. 'At the squat?'

'Yeah, of course.'

'I'm thinking of doing some again. You know, with paint though. The way I did then.'

She kind of glowed, all nodding, her pencil skidding about. 'A really great idea. Those pieces you did had exactly the kind of energy I'm capturing in you today. Such a sense of…connection.'

'You wouldn't mind? I'm inspired by you, see.'

'Of course I wouldn't mind. Why would I mind?'

I shrugged. 'Your turf and everything.'

'Not. Always been your turf, lil' darlface. And art is no one's turf, you silly.'

I licked the soft icing-stuff off of the ends of my fingers. 'Mmm…delicious—hey, I used to have a horse called Delicious Punk—well, my uncle had a horse called Delicious Pu—a racehorse I rode, see —in Ireland when—*oh!* I'm kind of chilly all of a sudden— gonna get my t-shirt—funny, you never know in August, huh?' I scooted past her, realised her unfinished drawing of me as her page caught my eye. I retrieved my t-shirt and knickers from the sofa, slipping into them en route back to the kitchen. She was leafing through her book, laying it on the counter with the pencil.

'We got some really good ones, my lovely. A few sales in there methinks.'

I could feel her gaze burning into me as I filled the teapot, fresh peppermint steam all belching up in my face. 'Ireland,' she stated, kind of weighty. I put down the kettle, my eyes skating up to hers. 'You never mention Ireland—that time you went. And you—are you alright?'

I felt the pull—in my heart—in my cells. I felt *him* like he was a part of me, wanted to feel him thus forever. I nodded, knew my eyes had gone glinty. 'I never loved him anyway. I knew straight away. But he had some kind of power over me. What was that? Some kind of obsession?'

'Who?' she said, a stutter coming through. 'Ireland?'

'Oh...no...' I rasped. 'No.'

'Oh—*that* him. Yes, I know. And you're well out of that one.'

'I had to go *that* far, huh?'

She held my eye, with a whole lot of love in it, murmured, 'It's okay.'

I sighed, nodded. 'I wonder if I'll ever truly love agai

       thrown wide open eyes open cunt open self ope

n?'

'You want to tell me about him?'

'Nah. Kind of. But I won't.' I held my hand against my heart. 'He's mine, se

       his kisses blur me into the ear

e.'

Her smile came through her nose. 'The one that got awa

       they suck me out of mysel

y...'

'Or not

       i am nothin

,' I said.

'Huh,' she said. 'What's in a nam

       and everythi

e?' She sighed. 'Yeah...what's in a name...'

We giggled together, all soft and sweet and secret. 'Does *he*—' my eyes flicked toward my room '—*your* one—kind of my one now, huh? But not really. I mean, I didn't mean that, of course, like—I mean your one—does he still mean anything to you, you think? We never speak of him either, do we, since that first exhibition of yours?'

'After all these years? Not really. I mean, yes, but only in the sense of a loving affection for the past and those that affected you in your tender youth. You know, I was—what?—a year younger than you are

83

now. My god, it was six years ago already.'

I nodded. 'I remember you saying…'

'I did have a deep and special kind of love for him though—you remember that, don't you?'

'Yes.'

'The one that got away,' she repeated. She held me in her golden eyes, a smile on her lips.

'Jessie,' I said, all sweetness threading through me.

She nodded, simple-as, and the space between us felt full of depth and knowing. 'I'm glad you have the collage,' she said.

'Me too.' I remembered how I'd felt like time didn't exist when I'd first seen the little image of the boy's cut-out face all floating in space. I remembered how I'd felt I knew him. 'Hey, you think we exist outside of our bodies?' I said. 'I mean—I don't really know what I mean—but, you know, a kind of bigger us, a bigger me— that's inside *and* outside of us at the same time? Is always loving me maybe?

'Well…I think it's possible. There are so many belief systems, huh? But I've always thought the soul is either inside the body—like when we're alive—and then leaves when we die.'

'See, I saw—the other night, when I was out of it—so maybe it was a kind of dream or hallucination or something—but it felt really real, Jessie, totally real, you know?'

'You saw…?'

'Yeh. So actually, what happened, see—and you know people say this really happens—I think I left my body.'

'You left your body? What, like astral projection, you mean?'

'Yeah. I think so. I saw everything going on from outside of myself—I mean, from up on the ceiling—saw myself and you and everything, and then I went above the rooftops and was flying, see, into the sky—and I saw a kind of me. And it was amazing.'

'What kind of a you?'

'Big me. The total Love-Me type-thing. Just like my uncle always would tell me—the old bastard—the whole of me, or true me or something. I was held in the densest love. Like the opposite of what was going on, of him and that drug fit. And I knew everything was going to be alright.'

'It was very freaky, from my perspective, for sure. I was scared as hell.'

'I know. That's what I mean: I had to take it *that* far, huh? But somehow it clarified everything. So—shit, I'm sorry—but now I've come to realise I'm glad, grateful, it happened, see. You being there was a part of it, a part of the safety and liberation.'

Her eyes were spangling with wet, holding me in a version of the transcendent love I was talking about. Mine sparked up in reflection. 'I thought maybe you were going to die.'

'I know. I'm sorry.'

She made a tiny gap between finger and thumb. 'I was *this* far from calling an ambulance.'

'I know...'

'It's okay.'

We stepped into a hug, all unconditional, just our two breaths and the depth of us together.

'Cake,' I whispered. And we chuckled, our jostling bodies warm against each other.

We took the teapot and cake through to the living room table. I cut into it, gave us each a massive slice, poured steaming peppermint tea out for us. We chatted about how delicious it all was, about art and the power of the mark, about colour and form, and what I myself might paint. And I was still going to act, I said. Why limit yourself to just one creative expression?

'I've been thinking...' I said, feeling myself all blushing up. 'About buying a flat. I know it's capitalist and all, and Eliot will about kill me, but...I don't know, it seems like a good idea. I'm getting such a fantastic wad for the perfume campaign and I want to do something with it—that matters, see?'

'Wow,' she said. 'What an achievement at seventeen, huh? Nothing bad about it.'

I felt the delight in my grin. 'Really? And I've been wanting to say, I'll get two bedrooms and you can come and live there with me. And you won't even have to pay any rent or anything.'

'That's really lovely of you. Of course I would pay rent.'

'Well, I wouldn't want you to—not when I keep making so much money.'

'I'm not doing badly myself.'

'Oh, I didn't mean it like that...'

She was smiling. 'I know.' She gazed at me, her hand on her heart. 'Well,' she said. 'There's something I've been wanting to tell you. I've been waiting for the right moment—and here it is, you've given it to me.' Her smile deepened, all kind of held in and spilling out at the same time. 'I'm pregnant.'

'Oh my god, Jessie. Amazing. Oh wow.'

'Yeah...huh? Who would have thought? And I'm so happy. It's thirteen weeks now. And Matt wants us to move in together. I think it's a good idea.'

'But yes, of course. It's the perfect thing to do.' I gazed into all her beauty. 'Oh Jessie. You're having a baby. Will I be the auntie?'

'*And* some.'

'That's so brilliant. And maybe I'll do drawings of you. All with your big belly and all. Not that I know life drawing—but you could teach me. Would you?'

'I'd love to. It's all about the looking.'

'I've noticed.'

'I'm sure it will come easy for you. I'd love to have you draw me pregnant when it shows. We could do the stages, huh? Hey listen— hold on.' Her chair sang across the boards as she got up, her voluptuous body moving easy as the lioness she looked like. The thought of her full of a baby was incredible. She took her sketchbook from the kitchen counter, where she'd left it by the open door, came back and flicked through its pages, landed on her object, turned it to face me. 'This one. It's the *one*. I want you to have it.'

'The *one*? You're giving me your best?'

'You give me your best. I've just got to colour you in with my coffee solution.' She laughed at her own words. 'Is that okay?'

All I could do was nod, like one of those little noddy doggies you put in the back of your car window. She drew the book onto her lap, tugged the drawing so it came away at the seam. She held it out to me. I took the leaf from her, gazed into the image of pure abandoned freedom my friend and I together had produced. There was joy in the crazy slippy kind of smile. Life, in her fast fluid lines. She had really *seen* me. And I was layered over words, loads of letters and fractions too, so it was all kind of like life, life unfolding and left behind, another letter, another word, another moment, another day.

There came a sense that all paths led home, although I didn't really know what home meant—was it The End? death? was it me? my Self? that Love-Me in space I had touched on my trip? I saw my assistant director had been a part of my journey and there were no regrets, right then, in that moment, and it was really weird but I kind of thanked him; a little flush of love coming all for myself, like it was spilling from the drawing in my hand.

My heart swelled, opened rose petal wings, this red kind of a bird all taking me easily *up!* and into life—into love and into pain—into a future I didn't know until it was *now* and it was happening. And beneath, came a subtle hum of a deeper energy, all coming from the pit of my belly it seemed, so I knew I was connected to the infinite field, a sort of exuberant dark emptiness from which all life flowed. And I knew I wanted to be here, in my life—knew I wouldn't sometimes too—but *right now* I wanted to be here. Whatever.

Printed in Great Britain
by Amazon